Destination Brides

Will the trip of a lifetime lead to the altar?

When Molly, Maya, Jenna and Eve bid on bucket-list worthy vacations at a charity auction, they each embark on the adventure of a lifetime at glamorous destinations around the world—but will they find love that lasts forever along the way?

Travel with them from the comfort of your armchair in

Summer Escape with the Tycoon by Donna Alward

Swept Away by the Venetian Millionaire by Nina Singh

Available now!

And look out for

One Night in Provence by Barbara Wallace

Available in August!

Eve's story by Liz Fielding

Available in September!

D0664349

Dear Reader,

Ciao! I was lucky enough to visit the beautiful city of Venice, Italy, several years ago. I still daydream about the magical time I spent there. The architecture, the beauty of the canals and the wealth of history all took my breath away. And the people were just lovely, so friendly and warm.

So the setting for Maya and Vito's romance brought back some wonderful memories for me. The two meet by accident, one that involves a tipping gondola! And they quickly find themselves falling for each other. But each has an internal wound from their past they need to contend with before they can move forward. Maya is in Europe to seek solace after a crushing betrayal. Vito refuses to forgive himself for his many past mistakes. Neither is looking for any kind of emotional involvement. But fate intervenes.

I hope you enjoy reading their story, as they fall in love in one of the most stunning cities in the world.

Nina

Swept Away by the Venetian Millionaire

Nina Singh

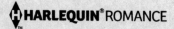 HARLEQUIN®ROMANCE

If you purchased this book without a cover you should be aware that this book is stolen property. It was reported as "unsold and destroyed" to the publisher, and neither the author nor the publisher has received any payment for this "stripped book."

Recycling programs
for this product may
not exist in your area.

ISBN-13: 978-1-335-49943-1

Swept Away by the Venetian Millionaire

First North American publication 2019

Copyright © 2019 by Nilay Nina Singh

All rights reserved. Except for use in any review, the reproduction or utilization of this work in whole or in part in any form by any electronic, mechanical or other means, now known or hereafter invented, including xerography, photocopying and recording, or in any information storage or retrieval system, is forbidden without the written permission of the publisher, Harlequin Enterprises Limited, 22 Adelaide St. West, 40th Floor, Toronto, Ontario M5H 4E3, Canada.

This is a work of fiction. Names, characters, places and incidents are either the product of the author's imagination or are used fictitiously, and any resemblance to actual persons, living or dead, business establishments, events or locales is entirely coincidental.

This edition published by arrangement with Harlequin Books S.A.

For questions and comments about the quality of this book, please contact us at CustomerService@Harlequin.com.

® and TM are trademarks of Harlequin Enterprises Limited or its corporate affiliates. Trademarks indicated with ® are registered in the United States Patent and Trademark Office, the Canadian Intellectual Property Office and in other countries.

Printed in U.S.A.

Nina Singh lives just outside Boston, Massachusetts, with her husband, children and a very rambunctious Yorkie. After several years in the corporate world, she finally followed the advice of family and friends to "give the writing a go, already." She's oh-so-happy she did. When not at her keyboard, she likes to spend time on the tennis court or golf course. Or immersed in a good read.

Visit the Author Profile page at Harlequin.com.

To my mom and dad, who made possible
my own many adventures.

**Praise for
Nina Singh**

"Singh's latest has a love story that will
make readers swoon, 'ooh,' and 'ahh'...
Snowed in with the Reluctant Tycoon is a
great read any time of year."

—*RT Book Reviews*

CHAPTER ONE

IF ONLY SHE hadn't left her packing until the last minute.

Though the chore did give her something to do, didn't it? A task to take her mind off the catastrophic events of the past forty-eight hours. The time period in which she'd gone from being a happily engaged fiancée with a set, determined future to a woman betrayed.

Maya Talbot tossed the sandal she was about to pack across the room in utter disgust. It hit the wall with an unsatisfactory thud and left a dark smudge on matte beige paint. *Ha!* As if packing was her most pressing concern at the moment. No, there was a much more tragic issue she was dealing with right now: the fact that she'd suddenly found herself single, heartbroken and sorely disappointed. All as she was about to embark on the trip of a lifetime. A trip her hardworking grandmother had been generous and kind enough to gift her. A journey that had originally been meant for two. And now she'd be making that journey solo.

It was all too much. Maya plopped down on the bed and sobbed into her hands. *How could you, Matt? How could you do this to me?*

But perhaps the better question was, how long had he been deceiving her? Exactly how many women had he betrayed her with?

A nagging voice in her head teased that, deep down inside, she had known. She had always suspected that things between herself and her fiancé were not quite right. She had to admit the trepidation she'd felt whenever the two of them began discussing wedding preparations. The utter lack of focus from Matt when she'd asked him to go over all the details. She'd put it all down to pre-wedding nervousness on her part and obtuse male disinterest on his. Clearly, she should have listened to her instincts.

This trip was one she'd often dreamed of being able to take. The fantastical trip she'd always referred to as her "bucket list" getaway.

All she'd ever wanted since taking that art history class as a university freshman was to be able to tour through Europe to witness the grand art in world-famous museums and to marvel at the majestic architecture within the most romantic cities in the world. It was all to begin with a stop in Venice. Followed by a trip by rail to Florence and Rome. Then on to Paris, with a final stop in the glorious metropolis of London.

Maya had talked about it so often with her grandmother. Through some miracle, Grandmama Fran had come across a charity auction being held in Martha's Vineyard where she lived. Bless her soul, the woman had dipped into her modest savings to bid on it for Maya as an early wedding gift. For a wedding that now would never take place.

Maya sucked in a deep breath. She couldn't do this. She couldn't go through with this trip; she had to have been kidding herself to even consider it. And there was not one other person she could think of to ask to accompany her. Working for her uncle's plumbing company as a contractor had left her with a severe shortage of female colleagues. And all her closest friends had gradually moved out of the Boston area over the years. Her cousins were quite busy with their own lives, as well—Lexie blessed recently with a newborn and Zelda immersed in a major project at work.

Unlike Maya, everyone around her seemed to be enjoying full, adventurous lives.

It was settled. Her mind was made up. She couldn't handle seeing all those glorious, romantic spots as a single woman. Not when the original plan had been so different. The only reason Maya hadn't canceled the trip immediately was because she couldn't bear to turn down the gift of a lifetime and have Grandmama's money go to such waste. It would have been bad enough for Matt's half of the trip to be a loss. Granted they would have shared hotel rooms. But all his meals, travel, and museum tickets had been paid for in advance.

But the more she thought about it, the less feasible the whole idea became. She just didn't have it in her. To traipse around Europe by herself, suddenly single and with a broken heart? No, she would stay here and try to pull her life back together. Beginning with somehow delivering the bad news of the broken engagement to Uncle Rex, Aunt Talley and her cousins.

Uncle Rex would be the toughest. He adored Matt and was going to be devastated. Not to mention the whole complication of Matt being the son of her uncle's business partner. The notion that she was letting her whole family down was hard to squelch.

The whole situation was one big mess.

She had to start with breaking the news to Grandmama. Maya owed it to her grandmother to explain exactly why she was essentially throwing away such a loving and generous gift.

Grandmama Fran would understand. She would have to. With shaky fingers, Maya reached for her cell phone on the bedroom night stand. This would be one call she'd never forget.

Her grandmother picked up right away. "Maya, dear. I was hoping to hear from you before you left. How nice of you to take time to call."

That was her grandmother. She was exactly the type of person to thank a grandchild for a simple phone call regarding a trip she herself had paid for. Maya swallowed yet another sob before trying to speak. "Hi there. I hope I didn't wake you."

"Nonsense. I'm much too excited to sleep." Her grandmother chuckled into her ear through the tiny speaker. "I know it's silly, but I'm as excited as if I were going myself. If only I was that mobile."

Maya found herself wishing more than

anything that could be so. Having her grandmother accompany her to Europe would be the ultimate solution to this big, painful mess. But Grandmama's various health limitations made any kind of travel impossible.

"I shall just have to live vicariously through my favorite granddaughter," Grandmama added, sending a spear of hurt through Maya's chest.

Dammit. She had no reason to feel guilty. It wasn't as if she'd been the one to cause her breakup. What choice had she had? How could she continue with a man who'd so utterly betrayed her trust?

None of that would make this announcement to her grandmother any easier, however. "Gran, I have something I need to tell you," she began with a shaky, soft voice.

"Oh, my. You sound quite serious. I hope you aren't about to thank me again, dear. You've already done so more than enough."

Every word Grandmama spoke was just making this endeavor more and more difficult. She should have prepared herself better, Maya thought.

Her grandmother continued without giving Maya a chance to respond. "I was so happy to do it for you, you know. You may think I'm joking, but you really are my favorite."

Maya couldn't help the smile that spread over her lips. Ever since she'd lost her parents, Gran had been one of the people to step into the sudden massive hole in her life where her family used to be. Sure, her uncle, aunt and cousins had all provided her with a substitute family, and she'd be forever grateful to them for that. But the bond she felt with Grandmama went far deeper than any other relationship in Maya's life. Gran had been as broken as Maya was over the tragic loss. The older woman's loving comfort had been the sole factor in pulling Maya out of the overwhelming grief and pain after the accident.

Maya wanted to crumble at the thought that she was about to deliver yet another, albeit much smaller, bolt of pain to the older woman.

"Thanks, Gran. I just…"

Grandmama jumped into the silence. "Are you sure you packed that red dress with the thin shoulder straps? You look so nice in that dress, dear."

This conversation was even more difficult than she'd thought it would be. Gran had actually been thinking of the wardrobe Maya would be taking. She really was living the trip vicariously through Maya.

"Oh, and it would go so well with those

strappy sandals you wore the last time you came to visit. This is all so exciting, dear!"

Maya bit her lip as she faced reality: she didn't have it in her to disappoint her grandmother. Not after the woman had already endured so much in her life. She just couldn't bring herself to say the words. Grandmama was so happy on her behalf.

Somehow, some way, she would make herself go on this trip. For her grandmother's sake if not for her own. Besides, who knew? Wasn't one of Matt's complaints about her that she always played life too safe? That she always took the path of least resistance? Not that she had much concern any longer about what Matt thought. But maybe he'd been right about this one thing. Maybe she would take this as an opportunity to try to be different, more adventurous. Going on a solo trip through Europe would certainly be an adventure. Maya decided she would do it.

Though misery was certain to follow her at every stop.

In all his thirty-two years as a resident son of Venice, Vittorio Rameri had never actually seen anyone topple out of a gondola before. He supposed it happened, though it was quite rare. He'd just never witnessed it firsthand.

That appeared to be about to change. For the woman he was watching as he sat at an outdoor table at his favorite waterside café was clearly about to lose her balance completely. Vito had no doubt she was American. Everything, from the tiny clutch purse she carried to the sensible capri pants she wore, tagged her as a young professional from a large US city. Maybe New York. Or Los Angeles.

He thought about going over to help but at this distance there was no way he would make it in time. He was right; it took mere seconds. The gondolier reached for her but the poor man wasn't quick enough. With an inelegant gasp, she toppled over the side and landed with a sharp splash in the water.

Vittorio blinked his eyes against the bright sunshine. She had to be drunk, despite the relatively early hour of the afternoon. He'd seen his fair share of tipsy tourists, and certainly wasn't one to judge. He'd just never seen one actually drunk enough to fall out of a gondola before. She'd attracted a crowd of onlookers as she splashed and spluttered in the water. None of them seemed to be of much help, however. The gondolier wasn't having much luck pulling her out, either.

So much for a nice relaxing afternoon.

He didn't know what compelled him to leave his much-needed espresso and the unread newspaper in order to go over and assist the lady. Perhaps it was the look of utter despair on her face just before she tipped over. Her expression clearly stated that she'd been through quite enough already. And that this fall into the murky Venetian water might ultimately be the last straw.

When Vito reached the gondola, it took extreme effort from both himself and the gondolier to manage to hoist her out of the water and onto the wooden walkway where the gondola was docked. She came out cursing in English. He'd been right about the American guess. Being fluent, Vito understood every one of the curse words she muttered. Or slurred, to be more accurate. Yep, she was definitely drunk. She was also soaked to the skin.

"Are you hurt, miss?" he asked when she stopped swearing long enough to take a breath.

He got a good look at her then and a strange sensation shot through his chest. Her eyes were the color of the Venetian sky at sunset. Thick, dark hair now clung to her face and scalp. Her makeup had clearly not been the waterproof kind.

Yet it struck him that she still looked quite lovely despite her accident of seconds ago.

The gondolier stood next to them, pale and silent. Vito couldn't decide which one of them looked more shocked, the boatman or the American. For an insane moment, he had to bite back the urge to laugh. He barely managed to withhold a chuckle. How rude of him. Her state was no laughing matter, after all. For all he knew, she could be sporting some nasty injury. She still hadn't answered his question.

She shook the water off her face. "Thank you for your help, whoever you are." Turning back to the boatman, she said in a surprisingly steady and deadly serious tone, "I've changed my mind about the gondola ride, sir."

That did it. Vito couldn't hold it in any longer. A small chuckle escaped him before he could stop it. She whirled on him with such force, he thought she might topple over again.

"You think this is funny, do you?"

Her golden hazel eyes blazed bright with fury. Fury directed at him.

"I'm sorry, miss. I certainly did not mean to laugh at you."

She continued to glare at him, despite his apology. The gondolier had apparently heard enough. Without another word, he jumped back onto his vessel and began to pole away. All too hurriedly, Vito thought.

The man had essentially just left him alone with this wet, tipsy American woman.

A woman who looked very good in wet clothes that clung to her skin. Vito gave himself a mental shake. Where had that wayward thought come from?

"You didn't answer my question," he reminded her.

"What question?"

"Are you all right? You didn't hurt yourself or anything, did you?"

She rubbed a hand down her face. Vito watched as the anger suddenly seemed to just melt away from her. Replaced by something akin to total resignation. With a jolt of surprise, he realized that made him sad for some reason. He preferred her angry to defeated. As if it meant anything to him. He'd never laid eyes on the woman before.

"I'm okay," she answered. "Just embarrassed," she added, glancing to the crowd around them which hadn't fully dispersed yet.

He waved a hand in dismissal. "Don't give it a thought. People fall out of gondolas all the time in Venice," he lied.

She studied him up and down. Her eyes really were stunning. A rich amber color that

shouldn't have worked at all with her dark
olive skin tone. But somehow it served to lend
her a rare and striking look that he couldn't
help but feel drawn to, given his artist's instincts.

He couldn't seem to tear his gaze from her
eyes. He tried to look away to avoid staring
at her face too long, but failed.

"Why don't I believe you about that?" she
wanted to know. The slightest hint of a smile
graced her full, pink rosebud lips.

"*Bene*. Perhaps because I've just made it
up."

Her smile grew. "Nice try. You're quite
the gentleman. First you come to my rescue
from a certain and tragic watery death. And
now you're trying to rescue my pride." She
glanced down at the soaking-wet fabric of
the red shirt she wore. It now clung to her
like a second skin and accentuated her feminine curves.

What in the world had gotten into him?
When was the last time he'd noticed a woman's curves? Certainly not in the last two or
so years. Not since Marina's accident.

An awkwardly silent beat ensued before
she stretched out her hand. "Thank you, Signor…?"

"Rameri. Vittorio Rameri," he supplied as

he took her hand into his. Her skin felt surprisingly warm for someone who'd just taken a plunge in dirty water. "I'm often called Vito."

"Hello, Vito. I'm Maya Talbot. From the great Commonwealth of Massachusetts. And I wish we hadn't had this very mortifying meeting. Nothing personal," she added after a pause, wringing out the tail of her shirt.

Oh, but he was so very glad that they had met. Damned if he could put his finger on exactly why that was so. He only knew that today was the first time in a long while that he'd felt drawn to study the features of a woman. He wanted to examine further the way the sunlight brought out the golden specks of her eyes, how the dampness of her hair took it to a dark shade of ebony that framed her delicate chin.

He wanted to think of how it would feel to sculpt what he was seeing before him. An instant desire to squash the urge rose in his chest. In his soul, he knew he wasn't ready just yet. Not to handle clay.

"I suppose I better get going back to my hotel," she said as he continued to stare. If she noticed the way he was looking at her, she was too polite to mention it.

"Are you alone?"

Her shoulders fell. The question seemed to deflate her even more. He found himself intrigued. What exactly was her story?

She shrugged and looked away before answering. "I'm afraid so. It's just me. By myself. In one of the most romantic cities in the world. Go figure."

Now that was surprising. By the looks of her, Vito would guess she wasn't often lacking for male companionship. "I see."

She dabbed a wet, trembling finger against his chest. "It wasn't supposed to be this way," she supplied. Vito guessed it had to be the alcohol that had her talking so freely to the stranger who'd just pulled her out of the canal. "I was supposed to be here with my fiancé," she continued.

"Uh-huh."

"But the…what do you call it? *Bastardo?* Yes, that's it. He was a *bastardo.* I learned that word from the hotel housekeeper who brought a complimentary bottle of valpolicella to my room earlier." She smiled at him.

Well, that explained the early drinking. Maya Talbot was a jilted bride. Or almost bride, as the case might be. But had she had the whole bottle? Still, he felt a twinge of admiration at the fact that she'd decided to come solo on a trip that had obviously been planned to include a romantic partner.

She twirled her fingers at him. "Well. Ta-ta. I should be going."

Vito reached for her arm before she could take a step. *"Un momento."* He couldn't just let her walk away. The woman was in no condition to be by herself in an unfamiliar city.

She blinked at him in surprise. "Yes?"

"Do you actually know where you're going?"

She blinked yet again before looking off into the distance to her left. Scratching her forehead, she turned to look the opposite way. It was blatantly clear she had no idea where she was. Let alone where she was going. "Well, I'm sure I can figure it out."

Vito weighed his options. Leaving her to her own devices was out of the question under the circumstances. For all he knew, she might actually trip and fall into the water again. He could offer to buy her a cappuccino at the café; clearly she could use the caffeine. But she was soaked to the skin. He doubted she'd be comfortable for long sitting in a wooden chair as wet fabric clung to her skin. Not to mention the attention the sight of her would attract from passersby. He could always load her into a *vaporetto* and send her on her way, but the likelihood that she'd get seasick was all too real.

Based on some past benders he'd been on himself, he figured the thing she needed the most was just to be able to lie down until the effects of the alcohol passed.

"Perhaps I can be of help."

Her eyebrows lifted over those dazzling amber eyes. "How?"

"My place is just over the bridge." He pointed in that direction. "We can go get you dried off and cleaned up."

She narrowed her gaze on him, suspicion clouding her features immediately. Not that he could blame her. She didn't know him from the street vendor selling gelato a few feet away.

"You expect me to accompany you, a man I've never laid eyes on before, to your apartment? Thanks, but no thanks."

He should have explained better. Fluency only got a person so far, it appeared.

Shaking his head, he tried to explain. "*Scusa*. First of all, it's not an apartment. I own an art studio near Le Mercerie. A public studio. Open for business. There's a comfortable sitting area complete with a sofa for browsing patrons. I might even have some dry clothing for you."

She looked him up and down. "I doubt we're the same size."

"I meant ladies' clothing."

Relief and understanding washed over her features. "Your wife's clothing, you mean."

Vito cringed inwardly at the word. Even after all this time, he hadn't quite adjusted to the new reality that he no longer had a wife. And he never would again.

He shook his head. "I don't have a wife. But my models have been known to leave things behind." Not that any kind of model had graced his space in the past several months.

"Your models? What kind of studio are we talking about exactly? Are you a photographer? Or some kind of artist?"

That was one way to put it, Vito supposed. Though, truth be told, he hadn't been any kind of artist in quite a while.

CHAPTER TWO

SHE'D CLEARLY BEEN dining on cotton. Maya tried to swallow past the dry ash that seemed to be coating her mouth and tongue. All she managed was a squeaky croak.

Water. She was in desperate need of water.

Maya forced her lids open and winced at the pain behind her eyes once she did. For heaven's sake. She hadn't even had the whole bottle. Just went to prove what a lightweight she was. After all, wasn't that a point that Matt had continually made? How often had he told her that she needed to let loose a little? To not be so constrained and proper all the time.

Maybe if she had done so every once in a while, her tolerance level would be a little higher.

Well, if he could only see her now. Sprawled out on a couch in what appeared to be the back room of an Italian art studio that she'd

followed a stranger to. She could hear soft
Italian voices from somewhere in the building. Two male voices and one female. Maya
didn't understand a thing that was being
said. She heard the sound of a door open,
then close.

Maya struggled to sit up. She wore a soft
cotton tunic of some sort. She vaguely remembered stepping behind a curtain to take
off her clingy wet capri pants and tank top,
nearly toppling over in the process.

But she also remembered other things.
Gentle, sympathetic chestnut-brown eyes.
Wavy hair so dark it had reminded her of the
moonless New England sky. A set of strong
arms steadying her on her feet after helping to
lift her out of the water. Who was he, exactly?

She really had no idea of the identity of the
man who'd brought her here.

A gasp escaped her chest. How utterly mortifying. She'd left herself at the total mercy of
a complete stranger. A stranger in a foreign
city where she didn't know a soul. No one
would even know to come looking for her if
this handsome artist man turned out to be a
cold-blooded psycho killer.

Maya bit back a groan. Definitely one of
the dumber things she'd done. But it wasn't as
if she'd followed the man back to his private

residence. Technically, she was in a public place of business. There'd even been browsers in here when they'd arrived after her drunken mishap with the gondola. Sure. Like that kind of reasoning would pass muster with Uncle Rex if he ever got word of any of this.

Uncle Rex. She hadn't technically lied to him and the rest of her family. She'd just bought herself some time, inadvertently doing the same for Matt. She'd concocted a vague tale about Matt running into some kind of emergency at work that would delay his travel and that he would join her in Europe as soon as he could. Just a small fib in order to postpone the nastiness that was certain to follow once she announced the demise of her engagement to the man her family considered to be the catch of the decade. Little did they know.

Little had *she* known.

Sudden tears stung the back of her eyes, exacerbating the pounding pain in her head. Fire burned behind her throat. All her earthly possessions for a drop of water.

The universe answered her prayers.

"May I come in?" she heard a masculine voice ask from the doorway. "I heard rustling. Figured you must be awake? *Sì?*"

"That might be one word to describe it."

Her rescuer walked in carrying a tray of assorted plates and dishes as well as a steaming carafe. But the only thing Maya could focus on was the glass pitcher of icy water with wedges of lemon floating on top.

"How do you feel?" he asked as he set his load down on the marble table between them.

How could she possibly answer that? So many apt descriptions came to mind. Embarrassed. Ill. Thirsty. Out of her element.

And to dig deeper, she was utterly confused as to what her future held now. A boring dead-end job. Her most significant relationship in complete shambles. Nothing to look forward to. She forced the thoughts away and focused her eyes on the man standing before her.

Maya had to suck in a breath. Now that her gaze had cleared, she realized her memory of their initial encounter had not done the man justice. He was breathtakingly handsome. Tall and dark, with broad shoulders and richly tanned skin. He wore dark pleated dress pants with a pressed collared shirt the color of the Cape sky at dawn. He looked like he'd just stepped out of a print ad for expensive men's cologne.

She pulled on the collar of her smock. Dear heavens, in contrast to this stellar specimen

of a man, she must look like a walking de-
molition site.

Without waiting for her answer, he lifted
the jug of water and began pouring into a
clear glass with yet another lemon wedge at
the bottom. So the man had mind-reading
skills in addition to killer good looks. Either
that or she looked as parched as she felt.

She took the water gratefully with a shaky
hand as she spoke. "I feel like I might have
drunk too much on an empty stomach and
then fallen into a river in front of a crowd of
strangers."

He gave a playful shrug as she took a massive swallow of water. The ice-cold liquid felt
heavenly as it poured over her thick tongue
and down her dry throat.

"Hey, these things happen," he said, giving
her a playful wink.

Maya wouldn't have thought she had it in
her to laugh.

Vito Rameri. See, she couldn't have been
too far out of it earlier by the canal if she
remembered his name. Though it would be
hard to forget the sole person who'd helped
her out of a situation like that. An artist and
a gentleman. Even the gondolier had taken
off at the first opportunity. Vito was the only
one who'd stayed to make sure she was okay.

Which begged the question: Had she even so much as thanked him yet?

She cleared her throat. "I don't know how to thank you, Signor Rameri."

He cut her off before she could continue. "Please. Call me Vito. Signor Rameri is my father."

"Okay. Vito, then. I'm not sure what would have happened if you hadn't come along." She studied her fingers. "I don't know how to pay back your kindness. I vow to find a way."

He waved a hand in dismissal. "Nonsense. Anyone would have done the same. We Venetians take care of the visitors to our city."

"Well, you shouldn't have had to take care of this tourist. Please believe me when I say that my behavior today was quite uncharacteristic. This isn't how I normally behave. I'm not even much of a drinker."

"Clearly."

Between his accent and the absurdity of this conversation, Maya couldn't tell if he was being sarcastic. If so, he had every right.

"I didn't think I'd had that much. Only I hadn't eaten anything since arriving yesterday and I guess I don't know my tolerance too well." Or lack thereof.

"Alcohol on an empty stomach can certainly catch up with someone who's not used to it."

She nodded. "Exactly. And I should have known better. It's just that I'm dealing with an unexpected…disappointment."

"Ah, right. The *bastardo*."

She'd forgotten about that tidbit in their conversation. "Yes, that would be Matt. My fia—" she caught herself. "My former fiancé. As of about three days ago." Though it seemed like she'd been dealing with the loss and betrayal for far longer.

Maya didn't think she could feel any lower. Between having to explain herself to this handsome Italian and the feeling of complete and utter rejection, her loser status was quite confirmed. And did the Italian have to be quite so good-looking? Why couldn't she have been rescued by a balding, older, grandfatherly type? Would that have been too much to ask? Instead, her savior had had to come in the form of a dark and charming Adonis clad in Armani.

Yet another way she'd failed at life. Another indication that she didn't fit in with the accomplished, overachieving family she'd been taken in by after losing her parents. Both her cousins had ideal careers and relationships. Her aunt was a revered professor at one of Boston's top universities. Her uncle a respected and successful business owner. And here she was, unable to enjoy a dream trip she couldn't have even afforded on her own without the assistance of her grandmother.

"Why don't you tell me about it? While you eat. You mentioned you haven't eaten since yesterday. It's just criminal to go without nourishment that long in a city with such gourmet cuisine."

Her stomach growled in response to his words. She studied the food-laden tray he'd set down earlier. An elaborate antipasto plate with olives, several varieties of cheese and small glass bowls of various dipping oils. A crusty loaf of Italian bread looked like it had just been pulled out of the oven. Maya's mouth watered despite herself. And bless the man, she could smell the rich aroma of strong Italian espresso wafting from the silver pitcher. In spite of the queasy roiling in her stomach, she really was quite famished.

"You shouldn't have gone to all this trouble."

"No trouble. I just stepped into the trattoria next door. I do it all the time." He motioned to the food. "Go on. Eat. The bread won't stay warm much longer."

Maya ducked her head. As much as she

wanted to indulge in the mouthwatering array of goodies before her, she felt like a helpless child who had to be taken care of. It was enough that he'd pulled her out of the water then given her a safe place to sober up. He certainly didn't need to be waiting on her, as well.

Not that the child comparison wasn't an adequate description. What she ought to do was to find her clothes, determine exactly where she was and make her way back to her hotel room overlooking the piazza. Then she should sit there and contemplate all the ways her life had gone so horribly astray.

Still, Vito had been so kind to get a meal set up for her. It would be rude to turn it down. "Only if you'll join me."

"I never turn down an offer to share a meal with a beautiful woman."

Wow. He really was a charmer.

"It will give us a chance to talk," Vito added, pulling up a chair to the marble table between them. "I get the feeling you could use a…how do you say…an ear lender?"

That tickled a smile out of her. "Close enough." She shook her head. "But I couldn't do that. I've already taken up so much of your time and graciousness."

He released a long sigh, one heavy with a

meaning she couldn't guess at. Lifting the carafe, he poured steaming espresso into both their cups.

"Trust me. At the moment, I have more than enough time."

Why exactly did he care? Vito really had no business wanting to know more about the sad American beauty currently sitting in his backroom office. But he found himself genuinely curious.

She called to him. Unlike anyone he could remember. Even Marina. A stab of guilt tore through his chest. Would he ever be able to think of her without the guilt eating away at him? Would her memory ever cease to tear him to shreds inside?

Across from him, Maya sat sipping her espresso. The way she seemed to savor each taste made him want to capture the expression on her face. His fingers actually tingled with the desire to find his sketch book yet again. Twice so far this afternoon, when he hadn't created anything in months. He couldn't remember the last time he'd felt that longing. No. Actually, he could. He could trace it back to the day his world had turned tragically upside down. And he had no one but himself to blame for any of it.

He realized she was speaking.

"I wonder if I should have even come."

"You were in no condition to go back to your hotel."

She bit down on her bottom lip. "I mean I shouldn't have come to Venice. I should have stayed home. In Boston."

"One should never regret visiting Venice."

She swallowed the piece of bread she'd bitten into. "Look how much trouble I've been. And it's only day two," she said on a miserable-sounding groan.

"Then we must assume it's only going to get better from here."

She grunted a laugh. The sound held no amusement. "It couldn't get much lower, could it?"

"Come now. Things could have been much worse."

Her eyebrows lifted. "How do you figure that?"

"Well, you could have been hurt during your fall. You haven't broken anything. By tomorrow, all of this will be forgotten. After all, I didn't see anyone with a phone out, filming or snapping photos."

The blood rushed from her face as she clapped a hand to her mouth. "Oh, my God. Are you sure? That would be all I need. To have all this posted somewhere online for everyone to witness."

"Including the *bastardo*?"

"Yes! Even him!"

Interesting phrasing on her part. Something tightened in his chest at the look of horror on her face. This former fiancé of hers had done quite a number on her. Despite his betrayal, she desperately cared still what he thought of her. The man clearly hadn't deserved the affections of such a lady. "Relax," he reassured her. "I was watching the scene as it unfolded. No one had any type of recording device."

Relief flooded her face. Then, to his surprise, she let out a small chuckle. "I'm guessing it was quite a sight to behold."

Vito bit down on his tongue to keep from laughing himself. She noticed his struggle. "It's all right. Go ahead and laugh. I won't take it personally."

He clasped his chest in mock offense. "I would never laugh at a lady in such a manner."

"I wouldn't blame you if you did. I'm sure I looked quite ridiculous as I lost my footing and splashed into the water."

"On the contrary, it was quite a graceful fall. Perhaps the most elegant instance of a lady tripping I've ever had the opportunity to witness."

"Somehow I doubt it. I'm certain it wasn't my most ladylike moment."

"I think being too ladylike is overrated, myself."

Her lips tightened. "So I've been told."

Indeed, he'd been right. The fiancé had left a mark on her psyche that would last for a long while. Vito felt a sudden intense dislike for a faceless man he wouldn't know if they crossed paths on the nearest bridge.

"I think you should forget everything this man ever told you," he ventured, though he knew he was perilously close to crossing a line. After all, he'd barely met the woman. For all he knew, her ex-fiancé was the love of her life. A loss she might never get over. Something he couldn't quite put his finger on told him that wasn't the case. Still, the tightness in his chest intensified. How silly of him.

"I'll have to give that a try." Her words were utterly unconvincing. She'd be licking her wounds for some time.

He wished he could find the right words to say, words that might reassure her, persuade her that this Matt wasn't worth the love she'd wasted on him. Even given what little he knew of the situation, he had no doubt the man had been given a gift and had been too selfish to cherish it.

As if that wasn't the most hypocritical thought, coming from someone like him, of all people.

"I wish there was a way I could be of help, *cara*," he said, dropping the endearment without thinking. Her surprised intake of breath told him she was familiar with the word.

"You've done more than enough."

"Yet here you are. Miserable and alone on a trip that was clearly meant to be a romantic getaway."

She slumped where she sat. "It was supposed to be so much more than that."

"Oh?"

"My grandmother won this trip for me at a charity auction. To raise money for a substance abuse shelter on Martha's Vineyard. She spent a good chunk of her retirement savings on my behalf."

And she felt guilty about that. His artist's eye could almost see it manifested. The guilt practically sat like a heavy, tangible weight on her shoulders. "Sounds like a deserving and noble cause."

"It was. She wanted the trip to be an early wedding present. A pre-honeymoon. Because she knew how much I've always wanted to see the historic art of the European continent. Matt would have never agreed to come if we'd had to pay for it ourselves. He's more a tropical island type of traveler."

"I see."

"It was such a generous gesture on her part. She'd tell me about all the marvelous trips she and my grandfather used to take. She wanted me to be able to experience something like it firsthand."

"Well, all I have to say is—better solo than never. Does that make sense as an American idiom?"

The pensive look on her face gave him the answer to that question. "I know what you mean," she assured him. "Nevertheless. I never should have attempted it alone. I've come to the conclusion that I'm going to cut this trip short. And stay in my room in the meantime. It was foolish of me to think I could enjoy this after everything that happened back in Boston. I've been kidding myself."

Vito couldn't help his next move. Reaching across the table, he took her trembling hand into his own. "I would be completely remiss as a Venetian if I allowed that to happen, *cara*. You mustn't leave. Not just yet."

"How can I let you leave this majestic city so soon? And without the opportunity to fully explore it?" Vito Rameri wanted to know.

A jolt of awareness flashed between them as he took her hand in his. For a moment Maya couldn't get her mouth to work. Electricity seemed to sparkle along her skin, originating at the exact spot where he touched her.

Once she managed to get her brain to focus, Maya wanted to answer him with a few questions of her own, albeit rhetorical ones. Questions like: How could she go on acting the happy tourist when her whole reality had just crumpled? How could she pretend all the activities she'd been so looking forward to as part of a couple would be anything less than awkward for her now?

Slowly she pulled her hand out of his gentle grip. She was clearly overcompensating for Matt's rejection. Looking for validation from a stranger. Sure, that stranger happened to be achingly handsome. Straight out of a romance novel. But she'd be remiss to start reading things into small gestures.

It was no wonder she was overreacting to the man before her. He was simply being kind. Worse, he'd probably taken pity on her. How pathetic that she thought there was some kind of mysterious current between them.

"I don't know," she began. "Day two didn't go so well."

"It's not over yet, however."

She supposed he had a point. And she could have done worse than meeting this charming, charismatic man. Though she would have preferred a much different set of circumstances leading to said meeting.

She watched as he poured more coffee into both their cups. What if they'd met under different circumstances? What if somehow she'd made this journey years ago as a single woman? Or perhaps with a bunch of girlfriends? She imagined wandering into his studio purely by coincidence, simply to admire a local artist's work. What might such a different introduction have led to? Would they have hit it off? She wasn't the type of woman to typically attract a man like the one she sat eating with right now. But maybe, just maybe, he would have seen something in her.

Who was she kidding? Vito Rameri probably wouldn't have given her a second glance under normal circumstances. It took literally falling into a canal for someone like her to be noticed by the likes of him.

She wasn't the striking, alluring type. In fact, it had taken her by surprise two years ago when the outgoing, successful, not to mention strikingly handsome son of her uncle's business partner had first asked her out. She'd almost been too stunned to accept his invitation to a leisurely pasta lunch in Boston's North End. To her further shock, Matt seemed to have genuinely enjoyed her company that afternoon. So much so that he'd asked her out again before their lunch was even over.

Maya had hoped she might have finally found the man who would help her create the kind of future she so desperately craved. A future with a family of her own. Not one she'd been thrust into after tragedy had left her orphaned and alone. One she actually felt she belonged in and fit into.

But she had to admit that, deep down, she'd sensed something wasn't right about the whole thing. Even on that first lunch date, the vibe between her and Matt had seemed forced. Rather than giving her the future she so desperately wanted, she'd known somehow Matt was going to let her down. Or vice versa.

Maya had ignored the warning bells that seemed to go off every step of the way. Those bells had morphed into all-out ringing alarms when Matt proposed. In many ways, he was too much for her. Too outgoing, too talkative, too *everything*. They'd both known and done their best to pretend not to. She'd also ignored her suspicions that she'd been nothing more to

Matt than a convenient way to present himself as a settled and serious career professional rather than the philandering party man
he really was. Again, she'd foolishly brushed
it all aside.

She looked up to find Vito studying her.
"You appear to have drifted off thousands of
miles. Back to Boston, perhaps?"

Maya gave a shake of her head. "I'm sorry.
Just thinking about some things, is all."

"I saw." He leaned back, inhaled. "Did anyone tell you that you have the most transpar-
ent face?"

"I don't understand."

"It's almost as if your features completely
alter as your thoughts do. It's difficult to explain."

As far as lines went, that was a new one. If
Vito was trying to come on to her, this was
the most unusual way she'd ever heard.

"No. I can honestly say that no one has ever
told me that before."

"It's true. Someone who creates art for a
living can see it clearly."

Yeah, that was definitely not any kind of
flirtation on his part. "Well, I think you may
be the first real artist I've met. No one's actually commented on my face that I can recall."

She saw his hand move ever so slightly before he curled his fingers into his palm. For an insane moment, she thought he might have been about to touch her. She imagined him trailing a finger along her jawline, cupping her cheek in his palm. A shiver ran down her spine.

The effect of his gaze was hypnotic. He wasn't so much looking at her as discovering, exploring her features. The air around them suddenly grew thick. In that moment, Maya had the strangest notion that she somehow knew this man. Had known him forever. She'd seen him in her dreams, heard his voice in her imaginings.

Or maybe she'd actually hit her head on the side of the gondola while toppling over the side.

"I have a confession to make," he stated. His tone as he spoke the words took her breath away. "I'm afraid you may not like it."

CHAPTER THREE

MAYA COULDN'T QUITE decide if she liked it or not. It was hard to believe what she was looking at. Was that really her depicted on the easel Vito had led her to?

He'd sketched her as she slept. At least, she thought it was her. For the woman portrayed on the canvas in charcoal appeared to be another version of herself.

"You're not saying anything, *cara*." Vito spoke softly behind her as she stood staring at the easel.

"I'm not really sure what to say."

"I will destroy it if you wish. We can pretend it never existed." The stiff quality of his tone told her clearly it would pain him to do so.

But was that what she wanted? Part of her felt flattered, proud that she'd provided any kind of inspiration to an artist of his caliber. Because he was clearly talented, given what she was looking at.

Another part, however, felt more than a little uneasy, as if her privacy had been breached when she hadn't even been aware.

She cleared her throat. "No. Don't do that. I just—I just need a moment to decide how I feel."

"That sounds fair."

"I've never been drawn by anyone before. I can't even really tell if it's indeed me."

"It is most definitely a sketch of you. Why do you not see it, I wonder?"

She scrounged for the words to explain. Maybe the alcohol was still addling her mind, but it was tough to summon them. "I don't know exactly. It's just that this woman on the paper...she seems much more...at peace with herself and her life. Confident in the decisions she's made." How he'd portrayed all that in one quick sketch was truly magical. She found herself in awe of his talent.

"This is my profession. As an artist, I capture what I see."

Maya trailed a finger along the edge of the paper. "And this is truly how you saw me as I slept?"

"It is how I see you," Vito answered with no hesitation.

Though it was flattering, she knew she couldn't read too much into his depiction of her. The man had laid eyes on her mere hours before. He had no idea who she really was. He didn't know any of the decisions she'd made that had led her to where she was right now—alone and licking her wounds. If Vito knew all that, he'd have drawn her much differently. Of that she had no doubt.

"If I may ask, what compelled you?"

"To put your likeness down on paper, you mean?"

Maya nodded. Surely he had better things to do, could have easily found a better subject. She had no doubt she was merely an inconvenience; the poor man had felt compelled to assist her as no one else seemed willing to. So she had no idea what his motivations may have been. She was far from muse-like.

So she was surprised with his answer. "You're one of those rare people whose inner strength can be seen clearly on the outside. It's a very uncommon quality."

Maya had to laugh at that. She couldn't have heard him right. In fact, none of this seemed real. Maybe she was still asleep on his sofa, having an alcohol-or concussion-fueled dream. Or perhaps she should go even farther back than that. Maybe she really had managed to injure herself during the fall from the gondola. And she was actually lying in an Italian hospital somewhere in the midst of a deep coma.

Dream or coma, Vito didn't return her laugh. "I see you find that amusing."

"Only because it's quite ridiculous. You obviously see something that isn't there."

"Or something you refuse to see yourself. Because you've let someone else convince you what's real."

Ouch. Served her right for confiding in a stranger. This random man she hadn't even known existed a day ago knew all too well about her humiliation. Maya felt her cheeks flame with embarrassment. Why had she ever left her hotel room? In fact, why had she ever left Boston?

The question made her cringe inside. She had to admit there was a very simple reason. She'd told herself that she hadn't wanted to let her Grandmama down, but the truth was that she hadn't been able to face her family after what Matt had done. She couldn't handle the thought of standing in front of the four most perfect people she knew to let them know that she'd failed. Even though none of it was her fault. Matt had been the one to throw away their relationship. She didn't want to admit that she hadn't been enough for him.

So she'd fled. And it had been a mistake to do so.

Because now some stranger was trying to psychoanalyze her. Irritation skittered along her skin. He may have helped her out of a sticky situation, but he had no right to try and read her or judge her in any way. She was beginning to wonder if she was some type of magnet for overbearing men all over the world.

"Don't pretend to know me," she bit out. "You really have no idea who I am."

"Maybe I know more than you think."

"Or maybe you're simply a heavy-handed alpha male who's much too quick to make blanket judgments about people he's just met," she snapped without thinking.

Vito chuckled. That made her irritation turn to anger. Now he was laughing at her.

"And why is that amusing to you?" she demanded to know.

"Because you're so clearly proving my point."

That was it, she'd had enough. She had no idea if there was some kind of language barrier that was fueling this agitating conversation. But she wasn't willing to participate in it any longer.

"Destroy the sketch or don't. I don't care.

But I think I should be going. If you would get me my clothing, please."

Vito studied her face before silently and slowly nodding. "Of course. If you're sure you feel well enough."

"I feel fine. And I'll find a way to repay your hospitality. I'm in Venice for a few more days." Only now that she'd said the words, she realized exactly what a difficult feat that would be. Now that the fog was slowly lifting in her brain, she distinctly remembered her phone and clutch purse falling into the water right before she'd gone over herself.

Which led to another embarrassing predicament. She had no idea how to get back to her hotel on foot. And she had no cash fare for any kind of boat ride.

She was at Vito Rameri's mercy yet again.

The atmosphere around them had definitely grown awkward. Vito knew he had only himself to blame. Obviously he'd learned nothing from all his mistakes of the past.

Maya was right. He was heavy-handed. And hopelessly incapable of sensitivity to others' feelings. He should never have shown Maya the sketch. Better yet, he should never have drawn it in the first place.

But when he'd come down to check on her,

she'd seemed so serene and peaceful on his office couch. The way her arm was draped casually over a plush cushion. The afternoon sun sending shadows along her skin. She really had looked like something out of a classic Renaissance painting. The woman had just been pulled out of the murky summer Venetian water and she'd looked none the worse for wear.

Though he was a sculptor by trade, most of his creations originated with a sketch on paper. Vito had taken one look at the tangled mass of hair framing her angular, patrician face and he'd felt once again that familiar yet so elusive tingling in his fingers. A feeling he hadn't experienced in more than three years. Not since the accident.

He hadn't been able to bring himself to ignore it. A decision he regretted now, given the way the *signorina* was glaring at him. He had no right to use her to grasp at a sudden and unexpected reprieve from the artistic block he'd been grappling with for the past three years. She was merely an unsuspecting passerby.

"I apologize, Maya. I should have known better than to draw you without your knowledge." In fact, he'd never done such a thing before. Never had he sculpted or sketched a human subject who wasn't aware he was doing so.

What had gotten into him?

He could venture a guess. Something about this woman was bringing forth an awareness he didn't want to acknowledge or examine. It made no sense.

Was it her sorrow he was drawn to? That had to be why. He felt bad for her. She was clearly hurting and lonely when she should have been enjoying one of the most beautiful destinations in the world.

She didn't look ready to accept his apology. In fact, she looked like she might be even angrier at him.

"You think I'm upset that you drew me?"

He could only shrug. If not that, then why?

"Never mind," she bit out. "I guess it's not important. Please tell me where my clothes are. And then I'll be on my way."

"Of course. I'll bring everything out. It should all be dry by now." It was downright silly of him, how disappointed he felt about her leaving. Or about how likely it was that he would never see her again.

"Thank you." She seemed to hesitate, looking up at the ceiling. "Also, can you tell me how to get to my hotel?" she asked after a long sigh.

"The easiest way would be by boat. You can catch one by the bridge across the walk."

"I'll have to walk. I lost my bag in the fall. Along with all my money, credit cards and cell phone." Her lips trembled as she spoke the words. She was clearly nearing her breaking point. There was no way he was going to leave her to her own devices under the circumstances. Particularly as he'd been the one to cause her latest upset.

"I can't let you walk back by yourself. It's already getting dark. You don't even know your way."

"I can manage. You've done more than enough."

She was certainly a stubborn one. But what did she expect him to do? Let her walk out into the night without a cent on her and no idea where she was headed?

How would he ever live with himself if his actions were even slightly responsible for the injury of yet another female? It was hard enough to live with himself as it was.

"Let me at least arrange a boat ride for you. A water taxi can get you right to your destination without any stops along the way." He held a hand up before she could argue. "I insist. I'll call while you get dressed."

Vito watched the internal battle as it played

out in her eyes. Her pride versus common sense. He breathed a sigh of relief when she finally answered. It appeared common sense had won out.

"Fine. If you insist. And I'm only doing this for your peace of mind."

Vito bit down on the amusement that bubbled up within his chest. To make it sound as if his arranging her transportation was a favor she was doing for him instead of the other way around. She really had no idea how magnificent she was. If she only knew.

And if only things were different between them, he mused. If only this charming, enigmatic woman who seemed to have reawakened his senses wasn't about to walk out of his life for good.

As quickly as she'd fallen into it.

She couldn't stop thinking about him.

Maya rolled over onto her stomach and adjusted the pillow under her head for at least the hundredth time since she'd crawled into her hotel room bed. She'd been certain she'd fall asleep within seconds after the harrowing day she'd had. And she definitely needed the rest. There'd be a long day ahead of her as she made the calls to replace her bank cards. She had no idea what to do about her cell phone.

But none of that had any bearing on why slumber was so stubbornly eluding her. It was because of him. Every time she closed her eyes, she saw a dark, enigmatic face with charcoal-black hair framing expressive, sad eyes.

She couldn't begin to explain it. Here she was, jilted by her fiancé, newly single after losing the man she'd hoped to spend the rest of her life with. But she'd barely given Matt a thought since she left Vito's studio. What exactly did that say about her? Or about the marriage she'd been about to enter into?

Vito said he saw strength in her. He'd challenged her when she questioned it. In response, she'd snapped at him and stormed out with barely a thank-you for all his efforts to help her. Now that she thought about it all, it hadn't been her proudest moment.

Maya sighed in resignation and slowly sat up in bed. It was no use. She wasn't going to get any sleep no matter how hard she tried.

In any case, she needed to update the folks back home about the loss of her phone and credit cards. Hopefully, the correspondence wouldn't lead to further questions about Matt. With no small amount of resignation, Maya propped open her laptop and logged into the hotel Wi-Fi network. After summarizing the essentials in a group email to her family and letting them know they'd only be able to contact her via email for a few days, she fired off a quick message to her bank explaining the loss of her credit cards. Then she called up the browser to do a quick check on various US news sites.

An email alert popped up immediately on her screen before she'd had so much as a chance to click on the appropriate icon. Her aunt. Maya should have known. The woman was constantly connected, mostly because she was constantly working. No real surprise there.

You lost your most essential belongings on the second day?

She'd included a laughing emoji but Maya had no doubt the response held a heavy dose of derision. Her aunt and cousins would never have been careless enough to let such a thing happen to them. Maya was the only one who had her head in the clouds. She no doubt owed it to her mother's genes. The woman had been a true free spirit, constantly in pursuit of one artistic endeavor or another. Her father had indulged his wife's less-than-stable career choices. Her aunt, uncle and cousins were much more practical. Bad enough they'd been burdened with the awkward and shy newly orphaned preteen. They'd been good to her; they really had. Still, she'd never felt the sense that she'd actually really fit in.

Maya typed out a quick response.

It's an amusing story. Will tell you all about it sometime.

She hadn't had a chance to hit Send before her aunt sent another message.

I'm sure Matt can bring a replacement phone and funds once he arrives. Honestly, Maya. How would you manage without him? When are you expecting him, anyway? We can't seem to get a hold of him.

Hah! She'd just bet Matt wasn't making himself available to her family these days. And Maya would have to discover quickly just how she'd manage without Matt by her side. To think, all these years she'd tried so hard to avoid letting her aunt and uncle down. Not to mention her two cousins. And now she was going to have to disappoint them about a broken engagement.

Maya wanted to slam the laptop shut and

launch it across the room. As much as she hated to lie to her aunt yet again, her shattered relationship wasn't the type of news one delivered via email from half a world away. The only thing to do was to ignore her aunt's question for the time being. Though Maya knew the older woman wouldn't let her get away with it for long.

Clicking back to the news sites, Maya worked to distract herself from all the jumbled thoughts scrambling through her brain. No wonder she was suffering from insomnia.

But that endeavor proved futile, as well. After a quick check on the Sox, her mind wandered back to the afternoon. More specifically, her thoughts returned to the man she'd spent it with. An image of the picture he'd sketched flashed through her mind. The idea that she might never see it again sent a surprising surge of sadness through her. She should have asked to keep it. As a way to remember all of this. A way to remember him.

But the whole notion was silly. It had been a simple impromptu lunch with a man she'd probably never lay eyes on again. Even if she did manage to somehow run into him before leaving Venice, they were from two different continents. Given the way she couldn't stop thinking about him tonight, she wouldn't need anything physical to provide memories of Vito Rameri.

Who was he, exactly? Any kind of artist prominent enough to have a studio in Venice had to be fairly successful. The flashing cursor on the search engine's query bar was practically winking at her, daring her to do something to find out. Without giving herself a chance to think, she pulled the laptop close once more and typed in his name with the word "art."

Now who was the one disrespecting someone else's privacy?

But what she was about to do wasn't really intrusive at all, she reassured herself. Technically, Vito was a public figure. He probably even had a large commercial presence online. She just wanted to see some of his professional works. To find out how prominent he was as an artist.

The answer to that was abundantly clear within seconds as her search returned pages and pages of results. To call Vito successful was a woeful understatement. Turned out that his creations were some of the most sought-after artworks in the world. His clay sculptures were in particularly high demand throughout the European continent.

Maya physically thwacked her forehead

hard enough that the skin actually stung along her hairline. She'd petulantly thrown a tantrum because a world-class sculptor had taken the time to render her likeness on paper. He must have thought her beyond childish. He probably also saw her as a completely ignorant fool. How many women would have been honored to be where she'd been?

Maya cursed under her breath and scrolled through several more pages. One article detailed the last renowned sculpture Vito had completed. The piece had sold for six figures at auction.

But something didn't add up. That article was dated years ago. About three and a half years, to be more specific. Nothing was mentioned after that. As far as she could find from this search, Vito's artwork hadn't been covered for the last three years or so.

The bottom of the screen prompted another link: *Rameri accident*. Something made her hesitate a split second before she moved her fingers to click on it. When she finally did, she had to suck in a deep breath. The headlines that appeared were vastly different from the write-ups about his art. The more Maya read, the more her heart slowly bruised for the man she'd spent the afternoon with. The sadness behind his eyes was justified, it turned out. Far from being the carefree, internationally renowned artist she would have pegged him for, Vito Rameri had a sorrowful past.

The pages she read now only told of heartbreak and tragedy.

CHAPTER FOUR

THIS WASN'T GOING to be the easiest conversation. Maya slowly walked toward Vito's studio, trying to summon the courage to say what she had to say. Best to just get it over with.

Yesterday the afternoon had been sunny and bright. Thank goodness for that, as she'd spent a considerable part of the day soaking wet. By contrast, that day's weather was overcast and gray. She hoped it wasn't any kind of indicator of the reception she was about to get.

But she had to talk to Vito. She didn't want his last impression of her to be one of a stubborn hothead storming out his door after he'd been nothing but kind and helpful to her.

When she reached the studio, she took a deep, fortifying breath before stepping inside. The man who stood up from behind the counter to greet her wasn't Vito.

"Buongiorno, signorina." He was tall and tan, with a wide smile and bright brown eyes. Upon closer inspection, Maya noted clear similarities between the two men. She wondered if they were related.

"I'm Leo Rameri," he said with a friendly grin, confirming her suspicions. Same last name. My, the good looks clearly ran in the family. "How may I help you?"

"I was hoping to find—" But he didn't let her finish.

"A readily available piece? I'm sorry. Vito has no inventory at the moment. I'd be happy to speak with you about a potential commission." His lips suddenly grew tight before he continued. "Though, I have to be up front and tell you that he may or may not accept the project."

He thought she was here as a potential patron. She didn't get a chance to clarify the reason behind her visit before the door opened behind her. Maya didn't need to turn around to know who'd just arrived. It was him. She could sense Vito's presence.

"Maya? Is that you?"

Maya took a deep breath before turning to face him. If possible, he somehow looked even more handsome today. He was dressed much more casually in a soft white cotton shirt and khaki pants, and his hair wasn't quite as casual. He'd combed it back off his face, lending him a rakish quality.

"You two know each other?" Leo asked from behind her.

They both answered at the same time, talking over each other. Leo came to stand between them, giving them curious looks.

"We met yesterday," Vito supplied.

"Vito was kind enough to help me out of a rather precarious situation. It's why I'm here. I realized that I should come back and thank him properly."

"That isn't necessary," Vito said in a firm, steady voice, his eyes fixed on hers.

Leo spoke before she could respond. "Wait a minute. You look quite familiar. Have you and I met before, as well?"

Maya was finding it hard to focus on whatever Leo was saying. She couldn't tear her eyes or her focus from Vito. He seemed surprised to see her. The only question was, was it a pleasant surprise or an unwelcome one?

"I don't see how you would have," Vito answered for her.

Leo rubbed his chin as he contemplated her. "Are you certain? Your face is quite familiar."

Maya made herself form an answer. "Unless you've been to Boston and we somehow coincidentally ran into each other, I can't imagine that we might have met at some point, Signor Rameri."

"Call me Leo. I'm Vito's cousin." He'd barely gotten the last word out when he suddenly clapped his hands in front of his chest. "It's you! That's how I know you. You're the young lady in Vito's sketch."

She could have sworn she heard Vito groan. "I think Maya might prefer if I destroyed the sketch, Leo. Or if it had never existed."

Leo whipped his head around to glare at his cousin. "What? How can you even think such a thing?"

Vito shrugged as he walked in and set down the parcels he was carrying. He motioned with his chin in Maya's direction. "The lady is unhappy with it."

She cleared her throat. "Now, that isn't exactly what I said. And that's part of the reason I'm here."

Both men gave her curious glances, then waited expectantly for her to clarify.

Maya should have better prepared herself for what she was going to say. Having Leo here didn't exactly help matters. It would have been difficult enough to try and talk to Vito without an audience. But she couldn't be rude enough to ask the man to leave his own cousin's showroom, now could she?

She cleared her throat. "I just wanted to come back and tell you that I feel badly for the way I left here yesterday. I should have been more gracious, especially considering your kindness and hospitality."

Looking at Vito's face became disconcerting as she spoke the words. So she glanced to where Leo stood staring at her. His mouth had formed a small O of surprise. Clearly, Vito hadn't told the other man about all that had transpired during her afternoon with him.

"And I shouldn't have taken the liberties I did," Vito responded. "We shall call dual *mea culpa*, then, Signorina Maya. And leave it at that."

Leo's mouth fell further agape. Based on his expression, he was clearly drawing some rather scandalous conclusions about what had happened between them.

"That sounds fair enough," she replied, trying to insert a lightheartedness into her tone. As if this conversation wasn't awkward in the least. "And please don't destroy the sketch." She wasn't brave enough to ask for it. It was a professional work, after all. Lord knew, she wouldn't be able to pay what an artist of his caliber was worth. "In fact, I wish I could take a picture of it to show the folks back home. But as you know, my phone fell into the bottom of the canal right before I did."

Leo suddenly held a hand up to stop her. "Wait. Wait a minute, *per favore*. Did I hear correctly that you fell into the water?"

She nodded. "That's right. Vito pulled me out."

"He did?"

"Mmm-hmm. Then he brought me back here to help me get cleaned up."

"I see." To Maya's confusion, Leo held a hand out to her. She hesitantly took it for lack of anything else to do. "You'll be joining us for lunch, Signorina Maya. My cousin has just brought back some mouthwatering pancetta and homemade pasta. I'm sure there'll be plenty for all three of us."

"Oh…uh… I'm not sure if—"

Vito interjected. "I'm sure the lady is too busy to drop her whole itinerary simply to dally around with us."

Leo wasn't having it. "I insist," Leo declared as he led her toward the back room where she'd collapsed on the sofa to sober up less than twenty-four hours ago. "I'm anxious to hear all about this fall of yours and exactly how my gallant cousin came to your rescue. Surprisingly, he's failed to mention any of it to me."

Maya found herself at a loss for words. She really hadn't seen this coming. But she had to think of something, some way to get out of this lunch invitation. Because if Leo wasn't aware of the murderous glare Vito was casting at him, she certainly hadn't missed it.

Vito Rameri clearly did not want her here.

If they'd been alone, Vito would not have hesitated to give his cousin a good, hard smack. In fact, he was planning all the ways he would deliver it as soon as he got the opportunity. The man was too nosy for his own good. He could give Nonna a run for her money when it came to busybody meddling.

It was bad enough that Maya had shown up here in the first place. She had no idea how hard Vito had been working to forget she even existed. How desperately he'd tried to put those few short hours they'd spent together in his rearview mirror so that he could continue moving forward with the steady existence he'd worked so hard to create for himself since losing Marina. He'd been foolish to mistake a fleeting bout of artistic inspiration for anything more. Her sorrow had called to him that day as he'd sat watching her from the café. There was nothing more to it than that.

But now he'd have to somehow endure a meal where she sat across from him, where he'd be required to look at her expressive face and notice again her flawless bone structure and features. After he'd tried so hard all these hours to forget.

"So, tell me about this fall you suffered, *bella*," Leo said as they sat. Vito focused on pulling out the food and serving plates. The steaming aroma of fresh pasta and fine Italian Parmigiano-Reggiano wafted through the air as he did so. Normally the enticing scents would be enough to make his mouth water. But today all he could focus on was the delicate flowery scent of lilac and rose from whatever perfume she was wearing. A heady mixture that seemed to be fogging his brain.

Maya ducked her head before answering. "If you don't mind, I'd rather not discuss it. It wasn't one of my finest moments."

Vito wanted to tell her she had nothing to be embarrassed about. But he could only guess what type of conversation that might lead to. He decided it was better to not say anything at all. Just get through this unexpected meal as best he could.

"Understandable," Leo assured her. "I'm

just glad you're all right. And that my cousin here was able to help."

He had to change the subject. "The sketch is yours if you want it," Vito said, handing her a plate of hot pasta.

She seemed taken aback; her hand shook as she took the food. "But I couldn't do that. After all, it's an original Rameri."

So she'd done some checking up on him. Her knowledge of his exact identity was new, he had no doubt. She'd had no clue who he was yesterday.

"That may be, but it belongs to you more than me. It's only right that you should have it."

"But why would you do such a thing?"

He shrugged. "You weren't a paid model, more of an inspiration."

She gasped. Now why had he gone and said that? It opened up a whole new slew of avenues she probably wanted to examine. And he had absolutely no desire to do any such thing.

Vito felt off, out of his element around this woman. It didn't help matters that his cousin sat watching the two of them interact as if he were a scientist observing a lab experiment. Yeah, Leo definitely had a nice hard whack coming his way as soon as Maya left.

"That's more than generous. I would never

have been able to afford any kind of original art under normal circumstances."

"It's only a sketch," Vito repeated.

"Nevertheless. It is indeed quite a generous gesture," Leo said, giving him a questioning glance and causing Vito's anger with him to spike even higher.

He ignored his cousin. "Don't mention it. I'll have my assistant prep and package it to be shipped to your Boston address. Be sure to give it to me before you leave."

She nodded slowly. "Thank you, Vito. Again."

Several moments of silence passed. Leo was the only one even pretending to eat. Vito couldn't seem to summon the appetite that had had his stomach loudly grumbling only an hour earlier. Maya was simply pushing her pasta around on her plate.

Leo was the one who finally spoke. "So, tell me, Maya. What are your plans for today? Will you be visiting some of our many historic sights?"

"Well, first I'll have to pick up an Italian burner phone. But yes. I'm scheduled for a sightseeing tour of St. Mark's Cathedral and the Doge's Palace. An exclusive guided tour for two. Only now the guide will have to settle for one." She wrangled a clearly forced smile that was just a bit too wide.

"Maya finds herself in the unexpected position of traveling alone." Vito answered the questioning look his cousin threw his way.

"Well, that won't do at all. We'll have to find you a tour companion."

Maya chuckled. "Oh, I don't mind," she said. Vito had to wonder if her statement was something of a fib. She sat ramrod straight, throwing out the words as if daring someone to argue with her. "Though I came very close to asking the housekeeping worker who came in this morning. But she mentioned it was her sister's birthday and she had plans. But I really don't have any kind of issue going by myself." She swallowed some water. "None at all." Again, the words were uttered with just a bit too much vehemence.

Vito had no doubt she was putting on a brave front. Yet again, a stab of anger at the faceless man who'd so callously abandoned her seared through him.

"Perhaps Vito might be able to—"

Vito suddenly stood before the other man could finish his sentence. He knew exactly where Leo was headed and had no intention of letting him go there.

"I should go back up front. It won't do to

have a patron stop by and find the counter empty."

The look Leo gave him relayed his thoughts just as well as spoken words could have. As if any real buyers had bothered to stop by the studio in over two years. There had been nothing available to sell.

He gave Maya a slight bow. "Please, stay and enjoy your meal, Maya. My cousin will show you out once you finish."

Leo's voice followed behind him. "Must you leave so soon?"

Vito didn't bother to respond out loud to the query. But the answer to his cousin's question was a resounding yes. Vito did have to leave. Because otherwise he might be tempted to do something he had no business even considering: he might foolishly offer to accompany Maya Talbot on her tour of Venice.

CHAPTER FIVE

Turned out Vito would be the one getting smacked. As he watched Maya step out the door less than twenty minutes later, he felt his cousin's open palm swat him across the back of his shoulder.

Vito had to clench every muscle in his body to resist the urge to hit him back. For, if he did, he would deliver a much harder blow than the playful one he'd received. And then things might very well escalate.

When was the last time he and Leo had actually indulged in a physical row? They'd had to have been teenagers. Nonna would throttle both of them if she ever got word they were fighting as adults.

Still, he had to wonder if the risk would be worth it.

He slowly turned to face the other man. "And what was that for, cousin?" he asked, with all the calm and steadiness he could muster.

"For being downright rude just now. To an American tourist, no less. One who was here as a guest at your studio."

"Through your invitation, let's not forget."

"That simply proves my point."

Vito sighed in dismissal and turned back to the newspaper article he'd been trying to read for the past several minutes. "You have no point. You're just a meddlesome pest who doesn't know how to mind his own business."

Leo wasn't taking the bait. "You're family. That makes you my business."

"Not when it comes to volunteering me to play babysitter to some lonely tourist."

"She's only here in Venice for a few days. What would be the harm in accompanying her?"

"If you're that worried about her lack of company on this trip, you should have gone with her yourself."

His cousin gave a sardonic laugh. "And try to explain to Lynetta why I'm spending the day with an unattached American tourist? *Dio mio.*" He physically shuddered at that possibility.

Leo came to stand right in front of Vito, casting his shadow on the article he was pretending to read. "Do you seriously think we're not going to talk about this?"

"About what?"

"About the fact that you haven't so much as picked up a pencil in several months let alone handled any clay. Up until a day ago, that is. When you sketched that young woman."

"So?"

Leo blinked. "So your sudden inspiration appears to have everything to do with the lady you just let walk out of here."

"She fell asleep in the back room. I simply felt a desire to capture her features. It isn't the grand breakthrough you're making it appear to be."

"Isn't it?"

"Not to me."

"That's mind-boggling. You come here every day simply to remind yourself of the life you used to lead, the passion you used to have. Someone may have finally revived that passion in some small way and you don't find it significant at all."

Vito slammed his hand down on the counter. "It's a simple sketch, Leo. Stop trying to turn it into some type of milestone. I'll know when or even if I'll be ready to create again. Trust me, this isn't the time."

"Not if you don't let it be. It's been three years, Vito. Surely that's enough time to at least consider moving forward."

"Family or not, I wish you'd remember what is and is not your place to try and lecture me about, Leo."

Leo's lips tightened as his eyes clouded with disappointment. "And I wish you'd remember that you were not the one who drove Marina's car over the rock cliff that day." With those words, Leo walked to the exit and shut the glass door none too softly behind him.

Vito bit out a curse. Leo was being downright belligerent. What business was it of his if Maya would be touring the basilica and palazzo on her own?

An exclusive guided tour for two. Only now the guide will have to settle for one. Her words replayed in his mind.

And what kind of guide would she have, he wondered. No doubt a distracted University of Venice design student who simply wanted the extra cash and was willing the day to be over soon. A random guide wouldn't be able to help Maya fully appreciate the historic art and architecture of the cathedral. He'd no doubt go on and on about lines and angles and historical facts that anyone could look up online or in a textbook. Such a shame and a waste of time for everyone involved.

There was also something else he didn't

want to think about. After the soulless tour, she'd be eating dinner by herself.

Vito gave his head a brisk shake. What did it matter to him? Again, it was absolutely no concern of his. He'd spent enough mental energy on Maya Talbot as it was. He already had too little to spare.

After buying an inexpensive phone, she was down to her last few euros. Thank heavens she'd left an emergency stash in her hotel room before she'd ventured out the other day. Her bank was in the process of delivering new credit and debit cards; she could only hope they arrived at her Venice hotel before she moved on to the next destination.

Now that she'd pulled herself together and had some time to think, she'd decided to continue with her European tour. The conversation with Vito and his cousin earlier in the studio had unexpectedly settled it for her. She might be alone, but she was going to try hard not to be lonely. After all, hadn't she decided back in Boston that part of her new attitude about life was to be more carefree? To worry less and do more?

Her fall had simply been a mishap, a bump in the road.

Maya cursed once again her monumental

decision to drink so much wine before her first-ever gondola ride. But if it hadn't been for that decision, she would never have met Vito. Her heart gave a little tug in her chest as she thought of him. No doubt she'd seen the last of the man. A man she would never forget. Maya would have to chalk their meeting up to just one more memorable experience on this trip. A teaser of what her life might have been like if she'd been born under a different sky.

Though, in some ways, maybe it would have been better if she'd never met him at all. It was so much easier to not actually know what one was missing in life. Maya sighed and slipped her newly acquired cell phone into her dress pocket, her thoughts still centered on the enigmatic, handsome artist who was sure to haunt her dreams for years to come.

So she thought she was imagining it when she looked up to find him approaching her from the other side of the walkway. She shut her eyes and gave a shake of her head before she looked again, just to be sure.

Yep, it was definitely him. And he was definitely approaching her.

"Vito?"

"*Buongiorno.* I was hoping I would catch

you. Luckily this is the only cell phone store within a mile of the square."

"But why?"

He shrugged. "Most likely because there isn't enough of a demand to warrant any other retailers." The hint of a smile at the corners of his mouth told her he'd deliberately misunderstood her question.

"If only more tourists dropped theirs in the water as I did."

"Yes, indeed," he answered with a small chuckle before turning serious once more. "It occurred to me after you left that you never did leave your address in Boston."

"My address?"

"Yes. So that I could have my assistant mail you the sketch."

Realization suddenly dawned on her. How foolish could she be? To think she'd even considered for a moment that he might have followed her because he wanted to speak to her again, to see her again. Although…he could have called the hotel for the information later.

Nonsense. Maya shook off that thought. The simplest explanation was often the right one. Vito only wanted her address so that he could mail her the sketch, just as he'd explained. She shouldn't try to find other motives simply because she wished for them.

"Here." He handed her his cell phone. "You can type in the information on my contacts list."

She did as he asked and handed his mobile back to him. Her fingers brushed over his, ever so slightly, and the same current she'd felt yesterday traveled down her spine and through her limbs. Whatever effect this man had on her, it was enough to make her tremble inside.

She quickly pulled her hand away, fast enough that Vito seemed on the verge of dropping his phone before being able to fully grasp it. Great. All she needed was to be responsible for yet another damaged mobile.

"Care to walk with me to the piazza?" Maya blurted out without thinking. What was the harm? She really wouldn't mind his company for a few more moments. Bad enough she'd be spending the rest of the day essentially alone.

Vito shifted from one foot to the other. He wasn't saying he would. Maya's heart sank down to her toes. She shouldn't have asked him, should never have risked it. Now he had to find a way to turn her down. So his next words surprised her yet again.

"It would be an honor and a pleasure to walk with you on such a beautiful afternoon, *cara*."

* * *

He was beginning to think he might have lost his mind. Vito had had no idea when he left his showroom to go and find her that he'd be spending yet more time with her. But there it was. Clearly, both her own question and Vito's response to it had surprised Maya, judging from the bemused expression she currently wore.

Except maybe part of him had known that his jaunt to the mobile store was simply a way to see her again.

There'd been no real need to venture out to find her. He certainly could have called her hotel later, asked about her address and wished her well with the rest of her travels. And the rest of her life, for that matter.

For some reason, he'd felt compelled to come and find her.

"I'd like that," she said with a smile. "I'd like that very much."

"Excellent."

He should have turned her down, told her he had things to do. So why hadn't he done just that? Damned if he could explain it to himself. Part of him blamed that busybody, meddling cousin of his. Leo had planted the seed, after all. Whatever the reason, it was too late to pull back now. Rather than dwell any further on his motivations, he offered Maya the crook of his arm. "Shall we?"

She took it with zero hesitation, her touch sending warmth up to his shoulder blades and down along his back. He was completely unprepared for such a reaction to a simple touch on his arm.

He didn't like it. Not one bit.

It was one thing to notice her physical qualities and want to capture them, given the artist in him. But this physical reaction was something else altogether.

Vito had to wonder exactly what he might have just gotten himself into.

It was ridiculous to be this excited. Maya made a point of reassuring herself that her overblown reaction to having Vito join her this afternoon was born of pure relief. After all, who would want to go sightseeing in one of the most beautiful destinations Europe had to offer all by herself? She certainly hadn't been looking forward to doing so. Thanks to Vito, her afternoon just became much more interesting.

"You are to start at the piazza? Correct?" Vito asked her.

"Yes, I'm to meet my tour guide there. Though I have a few moments to spare."

She glanced at her sensible watch. She had a much more extravagant one at home, with a gold band and jewel-encrusted face. But she'd never wear that one again. It had been a birthday gift from Matt. She gave herself a mental kick. She refused to think about him today. Or for the remainder of this trip, for that matter.

"Excellent. That will give us some time to enjoy the square."

A crowd was already gathered in the piazza when they reached St. Mark's. The line outside the basilica snaked back and forth. Dozens of gondolas and various other watercrafts dotted the canal ways.

"This is the busiest I've seen it since I got here," Maya commented.

"Pretty common for a Friday afternoon. Good thing you booked a tour," Vito remarked. "It's the only way to bypass the lines."

"I have my grandmother to thank. This really was the ideal wedding gift." Too bad the wedding in question would never happen.

"Your grandmother must think very highly of you."

Maya couldn't help the smile that formed on her lips. "She says I'm her favorite. Though I'm not sure how true that is. I think she simply feels a particular kinship with me."

"Oh? Why is that?"

"Because we both lost so much when my parents passed. She lost a cherished son. My father. And I lost my entire family."

"You're an only child?"

She nodded. "Yes. Though I grew up with two cousins. They're more like sisters, really. My aunt and uncle took me in after the accident. They raised me. I was fortunate that they stepped up."

"But you never stopped missing your parents."

A lump of sorrow lodged in her throat. She had to swallow past it before she could answer. "No. I think about them every day. And how much I miss them."

Vito stopped walking as he turned to face her. "Grief is a rather unforgiving monster," he replied. His voice had taken on a distant, pensive tone. His eyes darkened with emotion. And pain. Maya had no doubt he was speaking from firsthand experience.

She and Vito walked farther into the center of the square. A toddler squealed by them, laughing as he chased a pigeon then ran after another. His mother followed close behind with a genuine yet exasperated laugh of her own. The child nearly careened into a young, well-dressed couple sharing a chocolate gelato cone.

"You've lost someone, haven't you, Vito?"

He seemed focused on a point off in the distance. "I hope you don't mind my asking," she added when he didn't answer right away.

He gave a shake of his head before turning his gaze back to her. "No, it's all right. I'm just not used to being asked about it. This is a rather small city. Everyone already knows the story. It doesn't come up often."

Maya got the distinct impression that was most likely because he clearly discouraged it. Vito didn't seem like the type of man who took comfort from confiding in others. No, he appeared much too private for that. Too stoic. But something compelled her to press on. "Do you want to tell me?"

Pain and anguish were etched in his face.

"My wife. I lost my wife about three years ago."

The words confirmed what she'd read online. He was a widower. Vito Rameri had lost the woman he loved. And, by the looks of him as he spoke, he still grieved for her deeply.

She should not have pursued the subject. A virtual curtain seemed to close behind his eyes. The warmth and camaraderie they'd shared on their walk over had suddenly dissipated. She wasn't surprised when he quickly changed the subject as they approached the appropriate line for entry.

"Be sure to note the influences of other eras in the artwork," he reminded her.

"I'll try."

He gave her a small bow when they came to a stop at the place she was to meet her guide. "Enjoy your tour, *bella mia*."

With that, Vito turned and walked away. Without so much as a goodbye.

Vito didn't know how long he stood there, watching her from a distance. He tried to tell himself he was simply being conscientious, making sure she was met by her tour guide. He couldn't help noticing, however, that aside from an elderly man reading a newspaper and Vito himself, she was the only one in the entire square without a companion. And she looked nervous, shifting from one foot to the other. Despite her words at the studio earlier, Maya was clearly feeling awkward and out of place standing there alone.

But what business was it of his, really?

Vito told himself he should turn away, walk back to his studio and not give Maya Talbot another thought. The fact that he was even wavering over doing so was absolutely Leo's fault. That meddlesome cousin of his was the only reason Vito was even entertaining the notion currently nagging at him.

Leo's words echoed in his head. *She's only here in Venice for a few days. What would be the harm in accompanying her?*

On the surface, it appeared such an innocuous question. Perhaps there was no need to dig too far into it. Maya didn't know a soul in Venice. They'd met by accident and had gotten to know each other somewhat. Maybe they were even on their way to becoming friends. Truly, a genuine friend would try and help another out of an awkward and uncomfortable situation.

That's all this was, he assured himself. He made his way back to where she stood before he could give it much more thought.

She jumped when he tapped her on the shoulder.

The smile that greeted him when she turned around nearly knocked him off his feet. Maybe this hadn't been such a great idea. "Vito? You're back!"

He didn't often lie, but it seemed to be the best course of action at the moment. For the sake of her pride. "Leo just called me from the studio. It appears I've had a sudden cancellation of a previously planned appointment," he fibbed. "I find myself free for the afternoon."

Her eyes grew wide with shock. And pleasure. "You do?"

He nodded. "Since I'm already here, I wonder if I may take advantage of your extra tour ticket. That is, if I won't be intruding," he added quickly.

The smile she gave him was as bright as a sunny Venetian morning. "Why let a perfectly good tour ticket go to waste?"

He offered her his elbow. "Why indeed?"

CHAPTER SIX

IT NEVER CEASED to amaze him, the sheer wonder and awe on the face of someone entering the Basilica San Marco for the first time. Maya was no exception. Her jaw had been agape since they'd stepped through the arched doors. Her reaction could best be described as that of a small child experiencing her first amusement park ride.

But it was his own reaction that came as a bit of a surprise. Vito felt pleasure warm through his chest at the sight of her as she took in the majestic beauty surrounding them.

He'd been right about the tour guide. A disheveled and distracted university architecture student, barely out of his teen years. He'd introduced himself as Angelo. Now, as they entered the ancient church, the glances the young man kept throwing in Vito's direction were a clue that the student recognized who he was. Vito appeared to be making him nervous.

Vito wished for some type of miracle that might somehow have the whole cathedral cleared except for Maya and himself—including their distracted guide.

"It's breathtaking," Maya uttered, her voice barely above a whisper. But he managed to hear her. She was taking it all in with an appreciation so often lacking in foreign tourists. Not many of them appreciated the sheer genius of the artwork on the domed ceiling. The religious symbolism so craftily on display was lost on most.

Not on Maya. She could see clearly what a master work of art this whole building was. And she appreciated it.

Their tour guide was explaining the influence of Byzantine architecture on the cathedral and the religious importance of the mosaics. He then launched into the history of the artwork and when it was completed, what previous works the art had been influenced by. Maya politely nodded at his words without tearing her eyes away from the walls and the dome overhead.

Angelo continued to dart glances his way as he spoke. Vito wanted to tell the young man to relax. No doubt he was wondering why Vito Rameri, of all people, would be participating in a guided tour of San Marco.

If he only knew.

Maya sighed. "The pictures I've seen in various books can't compare to the reality of this place."

"Pictures can't do justice to a true masterpiece."

"No. They can't. I knew the mosaics were mostly done in gold but I couldn't have imagined the sheer luminescence of the effect."

Angelo interrupted them with a none-too-subtle clearing of his throat. "Should we continue on toward the apse?"

Vito motioned for him to lead the way and placed a hand on Maya's elbow.

Despite his own prompt, Angelo didn't move. He stood staring at the two of them, his gaze dropping to where Vito held Maya by the arm.

Great. Depending on who this young man's mentoring professor was, this little outing might very well fuel a fresh new round of talk among Vito's acquaintances. Vito wasn't sure he could deal with a gossip storm again. The last one had nearly destroyed him. He let go of Maya and dropped his hand to his side, clenching it in anger and frustration.

Angelo blinked and lifted his chin, as if summoning the courage to speak. Vito could guess what was coming and sought in vain for a way to head him off at the pass.

This was the reason he preferred to stay home.

"Scusa, per favore," Angelo began. "Are you not Signor Rameri?"

Vito merely nodded, hoping against all hope that the young man would just drop the matter once it was confirmed.

No such luck. Angelo thrust his hand in Vito's direction and spoke in Italian. "It is an honor to meet you, sir."

Vito had no choice but to shake the other man's hand. "Thank you for your kindness," he responded, reverting to English for Maya's sake. This was her day, after all. He had no desire whatsoever to make any part of it be about him. Angelo would just have to understand that.

For her part, Maya was giving them both a curious look.

"Do you two know each other?" she asked.

Angelo chuckled nervously. "Anyone studying art in Italy, or most anywhere else in the world for that matter, knows of Signor Rameri."

Maya turned to give him a look, one eyebrow raised. "Of course. How silly of me."

"If we could continue," Vito prompted.

"I would not have expected to be giving you a tour when I signed on for this job," Angelo said, obviously taking the hint that speaking English was the polite thing to do.

"Life is full of surprises." Some of those surprises were bigger than others, Vito thought. Some surprises came in the form of a vicious sucker punch and turned a once-content life full of purpose into a shattered mess.

"I knew I was right," Angelo continued.

"Right about what?" Vito asked, despite the trepidation warning him to just ignore the statement.

"About all the incorrect rumors. I argued to everyone who would listen that you were not, in fact, retiring."

Vito wanted to tell him it was none of his business. The only person his career concerned was Vito himself. Bad enough his cousin was a thorn in his side on the subject. Like he'd told Leo earlier, he would go back to work in the studio when he was good and ready.

"Retiring?" Maya asked.

"Why else would you be here if not for creative inspiration?" Angelo looked quite smug about his reasoning skills. He had no clue just how completely off his theory was.

"Rumors are the devil's playthings," Vito declared with a finality he hoped would compel everyone to just drop the topic.

But Angelo had still more to say. "No one can blame you for taking a sabbatical given everything that happened. I knew it was just a matter of time before you came back."

Vito cursed under his breath. This was why he kept to himself, why he didn't socialize or attend functions. His past always came up as a topic of conversation. One he had no interest in accommodating.

He should have known better.

Maya knew she wasn't imagining the tension coursing through Vito as their tour guide went on and on in a flat monotone voice. The stiffness in Vito's shoulders and neck was sure to cause one monster of a headache if he didn't let it loose fairly soon. She also hadn't missed the way he'd tried in vain to shut down Angelo's reference to his work or supposed retirement.

Whatever the exact story was, between her internet search the other night and all of Angelo's ramblings, she'd been able to surmise that Vito hadn't produced anything in a considerable length of time.

It had to have something to do with his wife.

To top it off, their tour guide hadn't been the only one to recognize Vito as they'd toured the basilica. Maya had caught more than one person doing a double take as they walked by. One young woman who'd been sketching in the apse looked on the verge of approaching him. Vito must have noticed her intent, as well, for he quickly walked in the other direction even as Angelo was still in the middle of a comment about a particular mosaic right above where they stood.

Now that the cathedral part of the tour was over, Vito seemed anxious to be out of there. She was feeling a bit claustrophobic herself. The crowds had multiplied since they'd arrived. At one point she'd found herself jostled badly enough that Vito had to reach over and steady her. She decided to ignore the little flip her stomach did as he placed his hands around her waist to keep her from careening into another church visitor.

"Shall we make our way over to the Doge's Palace, then?" Angelo asked once they'd stepped outside to stand by the lion statue. "Follow me."

He made a move in that direction but Vito held a hand up to stop him. "That won't be necessary."

Angelo blinked. "I beg your pardon?"

Maya's heart fell. Vito was cutting the tour short. He'd had enough. Though she shouldn't be surprised. He had definitely not enjoyed the tour. She'd have had to be oblivious and blind to not notice his discomfort.

"You won't need to accompany us," Vito added.

Wait a minute. It was one thing to be done with touring with her but it was something else entirely to send her guide away. This was part of her package trip. She began to protest but Vito interrupted her. "I can take it from here. We appreciate your time." He reached into his back pocket and pulled out a leather wallet.

The young man seemed taken aback but recovered quickly once he saw the wad of bills he was being offered. Maya waited until he was out of earshot before turning to Vito.

"May I ask why you just did that?"

He bowed his head slightly. "I apologize. I should have asked you first."

"But you didn't." She wasn't exactly miffed about that fact, but she would have appreciated being consulted on the decision.

"I can catch up to him and bring him back, if you'd like." Even as he made the offer, Vito's expression made it clear how distasteful he found that prospect.

"I'd just like to know why."

"A structured tour is so flat, so boring. You have access to the internet at home back in Boston, do you not?"

"Of course."

"And you are able to read books on history or art?"

She began to see his point. "Angelo wasn't telling us anything that can't readily be found in an art history textbook."

"Precisely."

"And I suppose you can make the rest of the tour more stimulating?"

He clapped a hand to his chest in mock offense. "You wound me. I think I can manage a bit better than a distracted, uninterested graduate student."

Did that mean that he was interested? In showing her around? In spending more time with her? Was there even the slightest chance that he'd sent Angelo away because he wanted to be alone with her?

She shook off the fanciful thoughts. Of course not; she was just foolishly searching for ways to mend her shattered pride after being duped by her fiancé.

Speaking of which, it came as a bit of a revelation that she hadn't thought of Matt in all this time. She should probably be missing him more, wishing that he was here with her. But he hadn't so much as crossed her mind.

That fact spoke volumes about her choice of a potential life partner. Then again, maybe it had more to do with the man smiling at her right now outside the cathedral.

Vito Rameri was definitely the sort to help a girl forget about other men.

"Well, let's go see if you can put your money where your mouth is, Signor Rameri."

He quirked an eyebrow at her. "Another American idiom."

Maya just laughed in response.

Moments later, they entered the historic museum that was once the residence of the Doge di Venezia. The artwork was no less breathtaking here than what she'd seen at the basilica. The entire palace was one monumental masterpiece with elaborate paintings on the ceilings and walls. Her senses were in overdrive; she couldn't decide where to look first. It was as if history had actually come to life around her.

She could sense Vito staring her way. How lucky was she to be able to visit these places with him by her side? A true native son who knew exactly how to appreciate the beauty and history that surrounded them.

Right. As if that was the only reason she was so thrilled that he was here with her.

"Well, what can you tell me about these paintings?" she asked him.

"Ah, *cara.* Don't you get it? It's about what you can tell me about them."

Maya turned to him in question. "I don't understand?"

"Tell me what you see." He reached for her then, and she could swear the blood stopped pounding in her heart. He touched a gentle finger to her temple. "What do you see in here?" Then his hand dropped to her collarbone, then lower to the area of her heart. "And in here?"

"Come, let's walk along the Grand Canal side," Vito said close to two hours later when they were back outside.

The tour of the palace had taken longer than she would have thought. But Maya would have spent days and days in there if given the opportunity. The visual magnificence of the venue was beyond anything she'd seen before. Now, as they stood back, Maya was still in the process of absorbing all the wonders she'd observed in both the basilica and palazzo.

"There's something else you need to see," Vito informed her.

Moments later they were standing atop a bridge around the corner looking up at yet another bridge—the arched structure that connected the Doge's Palace with another building—the *Prigioni Nuove*, the prison. Maya recognized it immediately. "The Bridge of Sighs."

"Another stunning work of Venetian architecture," Vito supplied.

That was one doozy of an understatement. The detail in the architecture alone was a sight to behold.

"The windows are so small. Why did they even bother with them?"

"Those poor prisoners from centuries ago had to have one last view of the city before they were doomed to incarceration."

"Yes. But it seems terribly unfair that the last view of Venice those poor ancient prisoners saw before being sent to their cells had to be through those small holes."

Vito rubbed his chin. "What else do you see? Look closely, beyond the basic structure."

Maya studied the bridge, squinting to make out the details. It was magnificent. But she wasn't sure what exactly she was supposed to be looking at. Then it struck her. Several ornamental carvings in the surface. "Are those faces?"

"Good eye."

That wasn't the first time he'd said that to her. Each time had sent a childish surge of pleasure through her chest straight to her toes. It had to mean something, didn't it? If a professional artist of Vito's caliber complimented you on your observational skills?

"They're meant to ward off evil spirits. And to guard the bridge as well as the two buildings it connects."

"As far as the prison goes, were the faces meant to keep evil in or keep it out?"

"That's the question, now, isn't it? I'm sure the poor souls passing through it on their way to their foul new residence contemplated that very thing."

Maya felt an involuntary shiver down her spine. Both the bridge and the jail must harbor the ghosts of angry and despondent souls who'd been sentenced to a term of misery.

Vito noticed her reaction. "Come now. Don't focus so much on the sadness of it."

"Hard to help it."

"Ah, but it isn't all doom and gloom. There's a romantic story linked to the bridge, as well."

"There is?" In all her readings regarding Venice, she didn't recall anything romantic associated with the famous bridge which led to dark and solitary prison cells.

"Certainly."

She would have to hear this to believe it. "Please, do tell."

Vito crossed his arms and leaned over the railing of the bridge they stood on. "There's a local legend that says under a precise set of circumstances, a couple that kisses under the Bridge of Sighs is destined for a lifetime of love and happiness."

Maya raised her eyebrows at him in question. She was definitely intrigued. "What are these circumstances?"

"That's the difficult part. The chances of all the variables falling into place are highly unlikely. Yet I hear it does happen."

"Oh?"

"See, if a couple can get it right, they can look forward to a bright and fruitful future together full of love and affection. That is, if they manage to time it so that they're under the bridge right at sunset just as the bells of San Marco ring out. If so, they will be granted eternal love and a lifetime of bliss."

"You're right. That's a lot of pieces that need to fall into place."

He nodded. "Adding to the uncertainty is the fact that St. Mark's bells don't even ring every hour. Still, couples do try."

As luck would have it, they watched as a gondola slowly glided under the bridge at that very moment. The two couples on board embraced and each shared a loving kiss.

"They've obviously heard of the legend," Vito remarked.

"Obviously."

"I don't hear any bells, though. Plus, it's not quite sunset."

Maya wasn't sure any of that mattered. Both couples looked like they were having the time of their lives.

Would she ever have that? she wondered. She realized now that she had never had it with Matt. Not for the first time since arriving in Italy, she couldn't help but wonder if Matt hadn't, in fact, done her a huge favor. Maya had no doubt he would have betrayed her after they'd gotten married. Once a cheater… and all that. Better that she find out and deal with it now, before she took his name. Or became a parent with him. She didn't know if she would have had the strength to leave him once she became his wife. Or the mother of his children.

Her gaze traveled to the man standing next

to her. It was hard not to compare him with Matt. On the surface, they both seemed to exude confidence. But when it came to substance, she had to acknowledge that Matt didn't have much of the genuine quality. She didn't know all that much about Vito but he seemed successful on his own terms. Whereas Matt had made never made a secret of the fact that he'd used his father's connections and clout as a businessman to get to where he was in life. Matt actually regarded that with pride. He liked presenting himself as the deserving son of a prominent and wealthy Brahmin family. Upon inspection now, she could see the image he wanted to create must have included a doting spouse.

In contrast, Vito seemed very much self-made. Everything he'd achieved, he would have had to do on his own. Professional artists couldn't rely on family connections. They either had the talent or they didn't.

Vito seemed deep in thought, as well. Deep creases lined his face; his lips had drawn tight. Maya had no doubt he was thinking of his late spouse. She had to wonder what she might have been like, what type of woman was able to attract the attention of someone like Vito Rameri. She must have been quite something.

Maya might have lost the future she'd planned. A development that had brought her to her knees several days ago, but one that she was gradually but surely recovering from.

Vito, on the other hand, had lost the love of his life.

Vito didn't know how long they'd stood there in silence, simply watching the steady flow of gondolas drifting under the Bridge of Sighs. In a scene that could have been straight out of a stormy painting, all too suddenly, the sky grew several shades darker. Clouds that Vito could have sworn weren't there mere seconds before suddenly burst open and released a torrent of heavy rain.

What the…? Nowhere in the forecast had there been any prediction of rain, let alone the downpour they currently found themselves in.

The shrieks of fellow visitors filled the air around them as they ran to find shelter. Maya was reacting differently, though—she was laughing hysterically, in a manner the Americans would call "cracking up."

"What exactly is so funny?" he asked with an answering smile of his own, once they'd run off their perch and reached the large umbrella of a flower vendor nearby.

"Oh, I'm just wondering why it is that the

fates have decreed that I need to get soaked to the skin every couple of days in Venice. And that you're certain to be around to witness the spectacle for some reason."

He returned her laughter with a chuckle of his own. "You know, the very thought had just occurred to me, as well."

"*Scusa*, flowers for the beautiful young lady?" the vendor was asking.

Vito didn't hesitate. He motioned to a wrapped bouquet of budding pink roses. A purchase was the least he could do; they were taking advantage of the man's shelter, after all.

Something told him he might have bought Maya flowers in any case.

Maya didn't say anything as he handed them to her. But her cheeks flushed a shade of pink not unlike the roses she currently sniffed.

"They're beautiful. Thanks, Vito," she said with a pleased smile, ducking her head shyly.

He hadn't forgotten the last time he'd bought flowers for a woman. How could he?

That particular flower purchase hadn't been quite as pleasant as this one. The day seemed a lifetime ago. But he replayed it clearly in his mind. He and Marina had had yet another heated exchange in a long line of chaotic and dramatic arguments—like so many that had plagued their marriage toward the end. Marina had snatched the bouquet out of his hands and thrown it in the bin.

Her voice, shaking with anger and disgust, resonated in his brain. *Do you think such a futile gesture would make up for the way you've been ignoring me for all these weeks?*

Vito pushed the memories away. What good was it to dwell on them now? He'd have plenty of time later, when he was alone. When he was sitting at his round wooden table in the apartment he occupied above the art studio, staring off into space and contemplating all the ways things had gone so horribly wrong in his life.

His gaze fell to where Maya stood admiring her roses. Her thick curls had escaped the sensible ponytail she'd shown up with this morning. Her eyes were bright, sparkling with merriment. Perhaps it was the artist in him but Vito could swear there was a visible aura around her. An aura full of light and laughter. He had to acknowledge that she'd brought both light and laughter back into his existence these past few days. A lightheartedness he didn't think he'd experience again.

Too bad it was all so temporary.

"I guess I should make my way back to the hotel," Maya said, interrupting his thoughts.

He couldn't let her walk or take a boat, as soaked as she was. "My studio is much closer, *cara*. Let's go get you dried off. Once again."

He didn't give her a chance to argue. He simply took advantage of the lull in the rain to take her by the hand and lead her back to his place.

"I'm having a profound sense of déjà vu." Maya wiped the wetness from her face after they arrived back at Vito's studio. "Only this time I'm much more sober."

So why did she feel so light-headed? Slightly dizzy? The afternoon had grown considerably darker. Shadows fell over Vito's features, the overall effect lending his face a mysterious, brooding quality that sent a small tremor down her back.

Vito handed her a large rag that he pulled out of a wooden cabinet against the wall. Maya took it gratefully and started to dry off.

"I can offer you refreshment of a more warming variety, if you're interested. You look like you might be chilled," he added with a playful wink.

She motioned to her wet clothes and did a little mini swirl. "You think so, huh?"

He shrugged. "Just a guess."

"I'm definitely interested in anything that may warm me up. What did you have in mind?"

He pointed to the ceiling. "I have an espresso maker in my apartment upstairs."

Was that an invitation? If so, was she prepared to take him up on it? His next question put her in the exact position of having to make that decision.

"You're welcome to come up there, of course," Vito offered. "Or I'd be happy to bring a cup down here when it's ready."

He was leaving the ball completely in her court. So what was she going to do? She didn't relish the idea of sitting down here in the darkened studio by herself. And she'd already spent an afternoon alone with him the previous day. Despite having just met him, Maya felt an unwavering sense that she could trust this man. Enough to be alone in his apartment with him.

"I'd love to help you make the espressos upstairs, Vito."

She didn't realize he'd been holding his breath until she watched the drop of his shoulders as he released it. What exactly did that mean? Probably nothing. There she went, trying to read into things again.

"Just one thing first?" she asked.

"What's that?"

She tugged at the collar of her damp dress. "Do you have any more of those smocks I might be able to borrow?"

Vito watched as Maya sat in the middle of his small, cozy kitchen, sipping on her espresso as if the cup had been sent to her straight from heaven. Her curls had all completely escaped at this point; the elastic in her hair had either fallen out or it was lost somewhere in her tresses for all he knew. Her cheeks had gone from a rosy pink to a deeper, more reddish color. The smock he'd given her hung like a shapeless curtain over her frame.

Still, he found her to be achingly beautiful. How the woman managed to look so attractive after getting caught in a rainstorm and while wearing a painter's smock was truly beyond him.

Whatever her appeal, it behooved him to ignore it. She'd be gone from Italy and out of his life in a few short days. Not that it would matter one iota if her stay here had been a permanent one. Vito wasn't at a point in his life where he could entertain any type of attraction to a woman. Permanent or otherwise. He had to pull his life back together. He had too much baggage, too much to figure out about himself and how he'd let the woman he'd married down so tragically.

Not to mention, Maya was pulling together the pieces of her own broken heart. The last thing she needed complicating her reality right now was a short and meaningless fling.

Vito sucked in a breath at the direction his thoughts had suddenly taken. A fling shouldn't have even crossed his mind. What was wrong with him? Was he desperate for female companionship?

He had to get a grip.

"I think the chill has finally left my skin. Thank you for letting me dry out, Vito. Once again. I'll have quite a repayment to make if you ever find yourself in Boston."

"If I'm ever there, I will take you up on that," Vito replied, simply out of politeness. He had no desire or inclination to travel outside of Europe at this stage of his life. If only he'd been able to temper some of his wanderlust before Marina had grown so fed up with his absences. Both his physical and mental ones. He'd not only withdrawn from her physically, he'd done so emotionally, as well. His only excuse was that he'd needed solitude and distance in order to create his art.

He made himself push away the useless thoughts.

"So, what's on the agenda for tomorrow?" he asked to try and change the subject before Maya could pursue any kind of questioning about the possibility of him going to the States.

She clasped her hands together in front of her chest. "It's quite exciting. I'm to visit a glass blower's shop. Followed by some shopping near the Rialto Bridge."

"Sounds like quite a day. And how about the evening?"

The excitement immediately drained out of her. Her eyes suddenly darted to the ground while a frown creased her lips. She fought valiantly to replace it with a smile, but the effect only served to lend a tight, forced set to her mouth. "Oh. That's to be another very exciting excursion." Despite her words, her tone was flat and rather empty.

Vito lifted an eyebrow in question. He could guess the reason for her poor attempt to hide her disappointment. The evening no doubt held another romantic activity meant for two. "What's the plan?"

Maya swallowed and nodded with enthusiasm. Too much enthusiasm, in fact. "Something I wouldn't miss for all the gold on the planet."

He'd guessed right. Whatever had been on her agenda, it was meant for a couple to enjoy together. He found himself reaching for her over the round glass coffee table between them, and taking her small, delicate hand in his. How could her fiancé have let this woman go?

"Tell me, *cara*. What is this exciting excursion you have planned?"

"One of the highlights of the trip," she repeated. "A sunset dinner cruise along the Grand Canal. Complete with champagne and authentic Italian gourmet cuisine. It was one of the activities that most thrilled me when I first found out about the itinerary."

Vito gave her hand a small squeeze. "Your fiancé is a fool of a man," he bit out, with more vehemence than he'd intended.

Maya sucked her bottom lip. "Thank you for saying that. Fool or not, there's no way I'm going to miss out on such an experience myself. Matt has no idea what he's missing. I thought I might ask around at the hotel to see if there'd be any takers for the extra voucher. You know, just so it doesn't go to waste. Not that I mind going alone." It was another clear instance of the lady doth protest too much. Vito kept that thought to himself.

"You have your heart set on this outing, I can tell."

She gave a small shrug. "Yeah, I do." He wasn't imagining the sudden sheen of wetness in her eyes. Vito didn't want to examine too closely the feeling that came over him at the sight. Pure anger and outrage on her behalf. "Not quite what I initially imagined it would be like, being alone and all. But still, an experience of a lifetime." Her lips trembled slightly as she forced a smile.

"I'm sorry, *bella*," Vito said softly, then wanted to kick himself. Maya was not the type to appreciate any kind of pity directed toward her.

Her next words confirmed that suspicion. "Oh, don't say that! I know how lucky I am to have this chance, regardless of the circumstances. How many people can say they've dined aboard a glamorous ship while sailing the Venetian waters? I refuse to let anything mar the experience for me."

She really was one of the most extraordinary people he'd ever met. Not many other women would approach the prospect of an evening alone aboard a romantic dinner cruise with such fervor and enthusiasm.

On the surface, Maya seemed upbeat. But Vito could see what was below the outer shell.

It was all clearly yet another act on her part. It was breaking her inside that she'd be experiencing such an activity by herself. Just like the tour earlier.

She leaned over and crooked a finger at him to come closer. "I have a confession," she said in a conspiratorial tone and followed it with a wink.

"What's that?"

"See, I made a bit of a resolution before I left Boston."

That had his curiosity piqued. "What kind of resolution?"

"I decided that I was done taking the safest route, the path of least resistance."

He blinked in question. "And what does that have to do with a dinner aboard a boat?"

"Don't you see? It would be so easy to just skip the whole thing. And sit in my hotel room, instead. The Maya Talbot of a few weeks ago would be quick to tell you that option is the one that made the most sense. But I'm done with easy. And I'm done with being sensible. Even if it means I'm the sole diner at one of those candlelit tables meant for two."

He couldn't be certain who she was trying to convince. Vito or herself.

"Does this resolution allow for partners, *cara*?"

She leaned back in surprise. "What do you mean?"

What, indeed, was he suggesting? Where was he going with this, exactly?

Damned if he knew. He just knew he couldn't stand the disappointment clouding her eyes despite her words of resolution and newfound bold spirit.

"I wonder if you might be up for having a partner along for this next adventure."

Maya finally looked up. She was staring at him wide-eyed. "Vito, I don't want to make a fool of myself by jumping to any conclusions here. Could I ask you to just come out and tell me what you're getting at?"

He gave her a small smile. "Well, *cara*, it's just that it occurs to me that it's been quite a long while since I've enjoyed a nice, relaxing dinner while admiring all of Venice's beauty from a boat on the water."

CHAPTER SEVEN

SHE'D BEEN HALF afraid he wouldn't show up. As much as she'd enjoyed the shopping expedition and her time at the glass blower's studio, Maya had been unable to tear her mind from the anticipation of the evening to come.

But he was here. And, dear heavens, was he handsome. Dressed in a finely cut tuxedo and polished leather shoes, Vito Rameri had every woman he passed along the walkway nearly swooning. Or perhaps that was just Maya projecting her own reaction onto others.

She watched now as he approached her while she waited to board the ship that would serve as their restaurant. He had his hair in the same combed-back style he'd had the other day. He hadn't shaved fully and now sported a subtle goatee.

She might as well have been watching one of her daydreams play out.

Who would have thought Maya would be

thanking her lucky stars for falling into these very same waters that day Vito had pulled her out. He stopped short when he reached her side. He smelled of spicy sandalwood with a hint of some type of mint. Maya resisted the urge to lean toward him and inhale deeply of the alluring masculine scent.

"Bellissima," he said when he approached her, looking her up and down.

"Grazie," she replied with a small curtsy. "You're not looking too shabby, either, Signor Rameri."

He held out his arm to her. "Shall we?"

Moments later, they were watching the dazzling lights of Venice from the deck of an authentic galleon.

Maya wanted to pinch herself. Was this all really happening? How had she ended up in such a stunning setting with this charismatic, charming and devilishly handsome man as her companion?

"This view is unlike anything I could have imagined. It's enchanting," she said, her voice sounding as breathless as she felt.

"Sì. It most certainly is."

Her heart fluttered when she realized he was staring at her profile as he spoke the words.

If only she were able to flick a magic wand

and make this dream part of a permanent reality somehow. But this was a fantasy, a once-in-a-lifetime magical evening. Even if, by some miracle, they lived on the same continent, Vito was a man battling demons. The vibes he gave off made it clear he wanted to deal with those demons by himself.

A waiter appeared beside them. He carried a tray with two full wine glasses of ruby-red wine. "Valpolicella."

They both lifted their glasses, then Vito tipped his toward hers in a toast. "To elegant evenings with newly acquired friends."

Maya felt a squiggle of disappointment in her center. If she'd harbored any illusions that any of this was romantic for him, that last word was a cold dose of reality.

She would choose to ignore his choice of words. Nothing was going to ruin the thrill of this evening for her. If she had to pretend for a couple of hours that this was a real date with her real boyfriend then what would be the harm in that? It would be her secret. Vito didn't need to know.

She tapped the rim of her glass to his and took a small sip. A burst of rich, fruity flavor exploded in her mouth. "Oh, wow. That's really good."

She took another sip, a little too hastily,

and some of the wine splashed out of her glass. She managed to avoid getting any on her dress, but a splash of it landed on the side of her cheek.

Vito chuckled and pulled the satin handkerchief from his tuxedo pocket. "Here." He dabbed the soft cloth on her skin, his face inches from hers. His touch suddenly turned to a gentle caress along her jaw.

"Vito?"

She knew she'd been the one to move first. But Vito didn't hesitate to respond. In the next instant, she felt his firm lips against hers as his other hand moved around her and down to the small of her back. His tongue moved over hers, the sensation sending shock waves through every cell in her body. He tasted of wine and mint. His heat suffused through the surface of her skin. Never had a kiss turned her insides to molten lava or had the effect on her that she felt right now.

It ended much too soon.

A sudden jostling of the boat pulled Maya out of his grasp and back to her senses. For a moment neither one of them spoke or moved.

Something shifted in the vicinity of her heart. It all suddenly made so much sense. Having Vito's lips on hers had set her nerve endings on fire. Had she ever felt such a jolt to her insides when Matt had kissed her? She didn't have to think hard to come up with the answer. With Matt, there had never been fire. Or any kind of electricity. She'd been fooling herself. She had to admit, once and for all, that the attraction to Matt had been more about finding a place for herself. In her defense, she really hadn't known. Not until now, when she finally had something to compare it to. Now that she'd met Vito.

Dear heavens. What had she gotten herself into? Maya struggled for some composure. She would take this experience with Vito for what it was. A magical, enchanted evening that had opened her eyes to what true passion really could be. As temporary as it was.

Vito stuck the handkerchief into his pants pocket and turned back to look out toward the city.

"Tell me, is the wine as good as the bottle you enjoyed in your hotel room the day of your uncompleted gondola ride?"

Maya ducked her head, trying to recover some semblance of control. "I have to be honest and say that I don't really remember. I didn't really bother to try and savor the taste of that wine. The point was just to drink it fast enough to flush away the harsh memories."

"Well, then we'll make sure you get to enjoy every drop of the wine you'll be served tonight."

"I will. And I'll make sure to enjoy it slowly," she said, reaching for some kind of normal conversation though she was still shaking inside, from the effect of his kiss as well as all the realizations that had come with it.

He nodded with a smile. "Quite slowly."

They watched silently as they drifted out farther into the lagoon. The palazzo and cathedral they'd toured just yesterday were both lit up majestically against the Venetian skyline.

"It's not difficult to see how a city such as this inspires such unforgettable art," Maya commented. The view before her would compel most people to try and capture it in some type of permanent way.

Vito turned so that he was facing her profile; she couldn't bring herself to look away from the city lights. "You really are quite visual, do you realize that?"

"So you mentioned. You said more than once during our St. Mark's and palazzo tour that I had 'a good eye.' To quote you directly."

"So I did. It happens to be the truth."

"Well, I'm going to take it as a compliment." She tipped her head in a slight bow. "Thank you, my good sir."

"You're quite welcome. And it's most definitely a compliment. Too many people sleepwalk through life without appreciating or so much as noticing the beauty that surrounds them. You are clearly not one of those people."

"I'm glad you think so." Though it didn't really do anything for her, did it? This talent she had that Vito seemed to want to point out. She was stuck at a dead-end job with her personal life in shambles. She would have much preferred a talent for recognizing lying, cheating scoundrels before accepting their marriage proposals. She still hadn't told anyone back home about her broken engagement. That thought gave her pause. She wasn't hurt anymore so much as angry with Matt. How dare he put her in the position of having to disappoint her beloved family? She'd worked so hard all her life to avoid doing so. Yet another realization that she wasn't hurt so much as she was angry.

"You're scowling," Vito commented.

Maya groaned inwardly. She refused to let Matt intrude on any more of this fantasy night. Her feelings for him were growing duller by the minute. As if he were some kind of distant memory of a past mistake she'd never be foolish enough to make again. Not now that she'd met Vito. She flashed him a wide smile. "Not anymore."

The moon appeared from behind a cloud and silver light fell over the surface of the water.

"So, tell me what you do back in Boston, *cara*. It occurs to me we never discussed how you spend your days."

Maya wanted to ask Vito to take back the question. She could still taste him on her lips. That's what she wanted to focus on right now. And the chance that he might kiss her again before the night was over. She didn't want to think about her ordinary, mundane, daily routine. This was supposed to be her fantasy, after all.

A fantasy which didn't involve her boring cubicle behind the front counter of her uncle's plumbing business.

"Tell me, *cara*." Vito prompted. "What do you do for a living? We can start there." Vito realized he was genuinely curious about her. His first impression of her as a jilted bride-to-be had gradually worn off and now he could see the dynamic and fascinating woman she truly was.

He wanted to know more.

"Let's see if you can guess what the answer to that may be."

"Ah, I am being challenged, I see."

"Let's see how well you do."

Vito rubbed his chin, not that he hadn't speculated about what career she might be in. "Hmm. Well, I recall reading in an article that Boston is quite the location for movie shoots. I believe several recent blockbusters were filmed there. Are you maybe involved in the film industry?"

Maya gave him a thumbs-down with her free hand and shook her head. "Try again."

"All right. I also know that several well-known international ad agencies have satellite offices in Boston. Do you work for one of them? Designing ad campaigns, perhaps?"

She gave him a smile that could only be described as sad. "I'm afraid it's not as exciting as any of that," she told him. "In fact, it isn't terribly exciting at all." Then added under her breath, "What an understatement that is." She must have thought he didn't hear her.

Maya took another small sip of her wine, deep in thought. Then she released a long, resounding sigh. "I do the numbers for a business my uncle runs. A plumbing business. I keep the books for him."

Her response took him by surprise. She didn't seem the type for an office job. Frankly, she didn't appear as if she could sit still long enough. But then, what did he know? How often would he have to remind himself that they'd literally just met a couple of days ago?

"If you don't mind me saying, *cara*, I can tell by the look on your face that you quite hate it."

"You are quite the observant one."

"So then why do you do it?"

Maya appeared to be weighing her answer. But before she spoke, the waiter appeared once more to announce they were to be seated for dinner. They followed him off deck to an intricately set table with a tall lit candle as the centerpiece. Vito heard Maya's gasp of pleasure as she took her chair.

He'd felt torn when he offered to accompany her. Her disappointment as she'd talked about having to miss this cruise had sent a mixed bag of emotions churning around in his chest. He didn't need to complicate things by spending any more time with her. But watching her earlier as they'd stood on deck sipping wine, and given her delighted reaction when they reached their table, he had no doubt coming here with her had been right.

It felt right.

Now that they were in the better-lit dining room, he indulged himself in studying her. She wore a simple red satin dress. But it looked far from simple on her. The delicate material hugged her feminine curves and accentuated her figure. The bright color did wonders for her olive skin tone and chestnut hair, which she wore in some type of complicated up-do that made him want nothing more than to take it down and run his fingers through her thick curls.

"I know I keep saying this, but this is all so spectacular."

So are you, was the immediate thought that came to his mind. Vito bit his tongue before he could say the words out loud. He'd learned long ago that empty compliments could sometimes do more harm than good.

One waiter set a large wooden salad bowl in the center of the table while yet another placed the first pasta course in front of each of them.

"I can't believe the sheer number of calories I'm consuming on this trip," Maya remarked. "I'll have to walk for miles each day to even come close to covering it. For the sake of my hips," she said with a small chuckle.

"You have nothing to worry about, *cara.*

Not as far as your hips go—or anything else, for that matter."

Now why had he gone and said that? He'd just warned himself to keep such comments in check. Maya's cheeks reddened to a color that almost matched the hue of her dress. Luckily, the sommelier appeared just then to pour them more wine.

Once they were alone, Vito figured he'd better get their conversation flowing again. To get past the awkwardness of his previous comment.

"So, you never did tell me why you stay in a position which makes you so unhappy."

Maya released a deep sigh. "I studied finance to help my uncle."

"With his business."

She nodded. "That's right. He had a bookkeeper who swindled him. By the time the crimes were discovered, the man was nowhere to be found. He'd finagled the books and embezzled a staggering amount of money."

"I see."

"For years after that, my uncle didn't trust anyone else to do his bookkeeping. He tried to do it himself. On top of maintaining the business. The extra responsibility really took a toll on him. He worked nonstop."

"So you saw to it that he had a bookkeeper he could trust."

"That's right. I knew he could use someone he didn't have to worry about stealing from him to help lighten his load."

Vito leaned over the table. "It was commendable of you to assist him in that way."

She lifted one elegant shoulder. "My uncle's done a lot for me. His whole family has. They took me in when they didn't have to. After I lost my parents."

"Isn't that what family does?"

She bit her lip. "Maybe. They could have let me disappear into the US foster care system. Some relatives would have done just that."

"So you felt obligated to become his employee."

Maya stilled in the process of lifting her fork. "What? No, I didn't do it out of a sense of obligation."

Her words surprised him. Did she not see it? "I'm sorry if I've made any kind of assumption."

"I did it out of love. And respect. My uncle stepped up when he didn't have to. He made sure I had a roof over my head and food on my plate."

"He sounds like an honorable man."

"He is. My aunt and my cousins, too. They gave me a family when they didn't have to."

Something about her history still wasn't falling into place. Vito couldn't explain it. There was a piece missing. He couldn't quite put his finger on it.

It occurred to him just as their main course arrived.

"It surprises me that you studied finance in the first place. Regardless of the motivations," he stated once the servers had left their table.

"Why do you say that?"

"It's not a subject that I would think matches your personality. Or your interests. You clearly felt compelled to do it for the sake of your family."

She quirked an eyebrow at him. "And you can tell all that after a simple sightseeing tour with me?"

Referring to a visit to two of Europe's most historic examples of architecture and classic art as a "simple sightseeing tour" was a bit belittling. She was getting defensive. Not the direction he'd intended the conversation to take at all. He simply wanted to know more about her. He wanted to discover all that he could so that he could form a strong basis for memories once she left Venice and walked out of his life for good. He wanted to know what made her tick.

He remained silent, waiting for her to continue.

"Not all of us have what it takes to become world-renowned artists, Vito. Being able to appreciate beauty and someone else's talent doesn't mean one has any of her own. Some of us just need to find a way to make a living and provide for ourselves."

Ah, no doubt she'd been told she didn't have said talent. Most likely by the family who took her in. Or perhaps some overbearing professor whose own failings clouded his judgment. Maybe both theories were true.

"Clearly you don't have to worry about earning a daily living," she added. "That would make you the exception to most of the planet's population."

He tilted his head in acquiescence. "I've been lucky enough to have chosen well how to invest what I earned from my commissions. Both in real estate and the financial markets."

"Most people aren't quite that lucky, Vito."

"I don't mean to overstep, *cara*. I'm simply curious about you."

She sighed. "You're right. I'm sorry. It's just… I did contemplate studying a more creative subject. I particularly liked an introductory art history class I took. I remember poring over the textbook. Particularly the pages on the European Renaissance. Showed it to Grandmama. I think that's when she first realized how much I'd love to see all the magnificent art in Europe."

He'd been right in his assumption. And judging by the longing look on Maya's face as she discussed the class from her student days, she still thought about her choice often.

"What happened?"

She gave a small shrug. "Nothing. That was the last of it. More sensible minds prevailed. The university didn't have a terribly large art department. And I didn't see enough of a future in such a field of study to do anything else about it."

What a shame. Maya seemed to have missed her true calling in life and appeared to have ignored a genuine passion in order to appease more "sensible" minds. And to pay back some sort of debt she felt she owed. To the very people who should have loved her without condition. He knew nothing of her family, but something told him she'd taken on the burden solely on her own volition.

She picked up her fork again with a sudden shake of her head. "That's enough about me. What about you?"

Vito suspected her desire to shift the conversation toward him was less about her curiosity and more of an attempt to change the subject. Maya was clearly uncomfortable discussing her missed opportunities.

He could relate.

"What would you like to know?" Hard to believe he was opening himself up to her questions. But turnabout was fair play, wasn't it? He'd opened this Pandora's box and didn't have the right to shut it when it was her turn.

"Tell me about your family. Leo seems quite charming."

Despite the lighthearted innocence of her words, Vito felt a sudden spear of dislike for his cousin. So Maya found him charming.

"He charmed one of the most beautiful women in Italy into marrying him. Lynetta is too good for him by half."

She smiled at his answer. "Despite your words, I can tell by your voice that you two are close. Your tone holds true affection."

And she'd called him observant.

"What about your parents?"

"They've retired and live in Sweden. I see them once or twice a year."

"Who else?"

Vito couldn't help the smile that creased his lips. "Then there's Nonna."

"Your grandmother?"

He nodded. "Yes. On our paternal side. Leo and I don't see eye to eye on much. But we both agree she's a force of nature." A sudden wish that Maya would be able to meet his grandmother surprised him. He had no doubt the two would get along fabulously. "We're heading out to see her tomorrow, as a matter of fact. A two-day birthday celebration as she turns eighty-five. Though you'd never guess. She's as active and sprightly as a twenty-year-old."

"You're lucky to have such a close family."

Did that mean she didn't feel particularly close to the family who'd adopted her? In her brief discussion of them earlier, she'd mainly referred to her relatives with a sense of gratitude. That had to be a terrible burden to bear as one was growing up.

"Close can often mean meddling and just plain annoying."

"He says again with yet another smile," she quipped, smiling herself. "Meddling and annoying would be worth it, to have such loving people who care for you." The longing in her voice tugged at his chest.

Vito started to reach for her hand across

the table but he was interrupted by another server carrying yet more steaming bowls of pasta. Just as well, he thought, leaning back in his chair.

The less he touched Maya Talbot, the better for his well-being.

"I know I'll never forget this night, Vito," Maya stated by way of conversation an hour after they'd finished their dinner. They were back up on deck. The galleon was on its way back to its port in Venice. She wanted to thank him for accompanying her. But the words didn't seem adequate. Besides, how many times could she thank the man for coming to her rescue in one way or another?

And she could no longer try to ignore the awareness that he evoked within her. The way he'd looked at her during dinner had made her insides quiver. Now, standing next to him in the moonlight in the crisp Venetian air had her senses in overdrive. His closeness sent a shiver down her spine.

Vito mistook her visible shudder for a chill. Without a word, he shrugged off his jacket and draped it over her shoulders. Maya snuggled into the fabric. It smelled of him, that heady mix of sandalwood, mint and man that had been tickling her nose all evening. The scent that had made it difficult to resist the urge to lean into him and inhale of it deeply.

"I'm glad you enjoyed yourself, *cara*."

Cara. She liked it when he used the Italian endearment for her. It would be one of the many things she would miss about him once this fairy-tale evening was over.

For it *was* nearly over.

In fact, her time in Venice and with Vito was coming to an end. The thought that she'd be on her way on the rest of her tour sent a deep sadness through her heart. How was the rest of her trip supposed to compare to what she'd experienced here in this magical city?

For that matter, how was she to return to her bland, boring reality in a couple of weeks when she arrived back in Boston?

"There's a term the Americans use..." Vito disrupted her thoughts. "I believe it's something along the lines of I'll give you a penny if you tell me what you're thinking."

Maya chuckled. "Close enough, Signor Rameri. I was just thinking of the past few days. And how spectacular they've been."

Hopefully, Vito hadn't caught the small hitch in her voice, the one that came from the knowledge that the end of this magic was near. In many ways, she almost wished she'd never set foot in Venice. Though she'd cherish this time spent with Vito for the rest of her days, her heart would break every time she thought of what she'd had for just a few short days in his company.

To think, all these months she'd thought she'd been in love. It was clear now, she'd simply been going through the motions.

Vito leaned over and pointed toward the city skyline. "Look at how stunning the cathedral is at night, the way it's lit up. Every structure around it serves simply as a backdrop to its splendor."

Hard as she tried, Maya couldn't really focus on the beauty that sat before her in the distance. Vito's shoulder brushed against hers.

She cleared her throat and grasped at some semblance of an appropriate response.

"Our visit to St. Mark's seems so long ago." Despite the truth of her statement, she remembered every detail of the previous afternoon. Including the questions that had been nagging at her. She took a chance on voicing one of those questions. What was there to lose at this stage of the game?

"Our tour guide that day, Angelo..." She paused, summoning some courage at the way Vito stiffened next to her at the mention of the young man. Still, she continued. "He seemed to know a lot about your career."

"I'm an artist in residence in the city. It isn't particularly noteworthy that an art student has heard of me." He shrugged but the gesture didn't quite catch the aura of nonchalance Maya was certain he was trying to project.

There was more to her question, more that she was trying to get at. He had to know it. "Angelo also had some very interesting theories about you. Your potential retirement, in particular."

Vito dropped his head to look down at the water below. "He was just speculating. People around here tend to do that about my career. It's quite irritating."

Maya ignored the insinuation that her own questioning was irritating him, as well. "Was he right?"

"About my retirement?"

Maya nodded, recalling the young man's words. "It seems that he was the only one of his peers who thought you were just in a temporary lull."

"I suppose that makes him right. It's true that I'm having a bit of a dry spell, that's all. I have no intention of rushing past it, however. Nothing is pulling at me enough to make my way back to my workroom."

She could have dropped the matter at that

point; his explanation was reasonable enough. On the surface. But in for a penny, in for a pound. "Does your dry spell have anything to do with losing your wife?"

His noticeable cringe made her want to somehow yank the words back into her mouth, to find a way to undo uttering them. She had no right to pick at the scab of his wound this way.

He must miss her terribly; the pain emanating from him made that abundantly clear. If there was a way to somehow take that pain away, to ease his anguish, Maya would have happily provided it.

But she couldn't bring his love back. Nothing could.

"It's been over three years since her accident," Vito said. His voice was surprisingly flat, as if he were spouting some meaningless statistic.

"It takes more than three years to lessen such pain."

He nodded slowly, his gaze still focused on the bright lights of the approaching city.

"Indeed it does. Particularly when the pain is so intricately intertwined with guilt for one's role in causing said pain."

"It's natural to feel some responsibility after a tragedy—"

He cut her off before she could continue. "Oh, but I do bear the responsibility. It's so much more than just a feeling on my part."

Maya's mouth went dry at the implication of his words. Vito made it sound as if he'd had a direct hand in his wife's accident. His hands clenched into tight fists over the railing. "I don't understand."

"It isn't terribly complicated," he answered, his voice rasping and thick. "See, if she hadn't married me, Marina would still be alive and well."

CHAPTER EIGHT

EVEN AFTER THEY'D docked and disembarked, Maya still hadn't quite found her voice. She'd been afraid to say anything after Vito made his stunning declaration. So she'd stayed silent, giving him the time and opportunity to clarify or explain.

So far, he hadn't.

Nor did he seem inclined to do so, Maya noticed, as he helped her step off the boat and onto the wooden boardwalk.

This was all wrong. It was their last night together; their time spent in each other's company couldn't be ending on such a mysterious and loaded note. Maya placed a gentle hand on his arm as they approached the center of the square. Even under the current circumstance, the heat of his skin under his silk shirt caused a warm sensation to travel up her arm. Maya still wore his tuxedo jacket.

"Vito, I'd really like to talk."

He rubbed a hand down his face. "About what I said on the boat regarding my wife's accident."

She nodded, but they didn't get a chance to continue the conversation. A female voice suddenly called through the night air.

"Vito!"

Maya turned to see a tall, statuesque woman in a flowing white lace spring dress approaching the two of them, her arms out-stretched and a wide smile gracing her strik-ingly pretty face. Hard on her heels was Leo. For his part, Vito's cousin seemed quite sur-prised to see them.

Vito's quiet groan wasn't low enough that she didn't hear it. He was far from thrilled to see these two.

The other couple reached them seconds later. The lady threw her arms around Vito's neck and he returned her embrace with one of his own. There was no hint of flirtation or attraction. Simply genuine affection.

This had to be Leo's wife.

"What a surprise to see you here, cousin." Leo spoke in English. "And with Maya by your side." He eyed the two of them up and down.

"A bit dressed up, aren't you?"

Lynetta didn't let them answer. "This must be the lovely American lady Leo's been telling me about." She jabbed her husband playfully in the ribs. "You didn't mention how pretty she was."

Coming from someone who looked the way she did, that was quite the compliment.

"Very glad to meet you," Maya said, extending her hand. But Lynetta ignored it. Instead, she threw her arms around Maya's shoulders and planted a kiss on each cheek.

"I'm so happy we ran into you before you left our beautiful city." Lynetta's accent, though subtle, lent another layer of charisma to her ample charm.

She crooked her hand through Maya's arm. "Come, let's walk a bit."

Maya cast a hesitant glance in Vito's direction. His cousin still had his full attention. They were discussing something in Italian. Leo was quite animated. She could have sworn she heard her name thrown about at least twice.

Lynetta led them farther toward the square. By the time the men had caught up to them, Maya had heard all about the couple's two toddler sons and how she and her husband had managed to sneak out for a quick drink thanks to the teenager who babysat for them occasionally.

"We can't make it too late a night, however," Lynetta now added. "We are traveling early tomorrow to Verona. To celebrate Vito and Leo's grandmother's birthday."

"Yes, Vito mentioned that earlier this evening. Please wish your grandmother a happy eighty-fifth. I hope she has a lovely time with her family."

"What have you got planned for tomorrow, dear?" Lynetta asked. "Any excursions through our beautiful city?"

Maya shook her head. "It happens to be a free day. Nothing on the agenda. I think I'll take the time to just relax in my hotel room. Or maybe do a walking tour."

Lynetta blinked at her. "By yourself?"

Maya had to laugh at her tone. She sounded as if Maya would be walking across that prisoners' bridge by the palazzo on her way to a cell rather than strolling through the beautiful streets of Venice.

"I'm sure I'll find plenty to do."

The other woman stopped pacing. "Tell me, Maya. Do you have plans to visit Verona?"

Maya shook her head. "It isn't one of the destinations on this trip. From here, I'm off to Florence. Then Rome."

Lynetta clasped her hands in front of her chest. "That settles it, then. You must come with us."

Maya sensed more than heard Vito's sharp intake of breath behind them. "Lynetta!"

The other woman whirled to face him, bit something out in Italian. Then added in English, "And don't you dare take that tone of voice with me. It was rude of you not to invite her yourself."

Maya held out a hand to interject. "Please. I don't want to intrude where I don't belong."

It was her turn to face Lynetta's harsh glare. "Are you turning down my invitation? To an old lady's birthday gathering?"

Maya found she couldn't find the words to reply. The way Lynetta posed the question, she sounded like Maya was committing a dire faux pas by declining. Never mind that Vito stood slack-jawed, watching this unexpected development unfold without saying a thing. If he'd wanted her at his grandmother's birthday, he would have invited her himself.

Not that she'd even wanted the invitation. Had she?

Maya felt a flush of embarrassment and confusion creep up on her cheeks. The whole situation had somehow gotten out of hand. It didn't help matters that Leo was chuckling softly as he watched the three of them.

"But I couldn't possibly intrude that way," Maya repeated, stumbling over the words.

"I'm sure the travel has all been prearranged and everyone's tickets already purchased."

Lynetta's glare softened. "Don't be silly, dear. It's not an intrusion. Nonna would love to have you there. She loves America and would quite enjoy an American visitor. As for as any type of ticket, we'll be traveling on Vito's private aircraft."

So much for any kind of practical excuse. Vito suddenly stepped in front of her.

"Please excuse my cousin-in-law's domineering attitude, Maya. She can't help herself."

From behind him, Lynetta gave Vito a firm swat on his upper arm. He ignored her. "Additionally, I would love it if you'd accompany the three of us, along with my two nephews, to Nonna's birthday celebration in Verona."

Maya wasn't going to delude herself. Vito clearly felt obliged to extend the invitation. He must have felt like he had no choice after what Lynetta had started. Maya knew his motives for offering the invite had nothing to do with wanting to spend time with her. Lynetta had simply forced his hand.

So why was she so tempted to accept it?

"Well, it's settled, then," his meddlesome cousin-in-law stated with finality before

Maya had even had a chance to respond. "Let's celebrate with some gelato in the square, shall we?" Lynetta continued. "Vito, as usual, you'll be buying."

He let the two women walk ahead once more but stopped Leo before he could move. "What the hell has your wife just done?"

Leo actually laughed. Why was Vito surprised? Why had he even expected some hint of sympathy from the other man?

"Why, I believe she's just done you a favor. And now you can thank her with some chocolate gelato."

Vito tilted his head back and took a deep breath to calm down. "Is that really how you see this disastrous development?"

Leo squinted at him. "Why not? You're actually out with her right now. You two have clearly just enjoyed some kind of date. Taking her to Nonna's would simply be an extension, wouldn't it?"

"We weren't on any kind of date, Leo."

Leo eyed Vito's pressed tuxedo pants and the white silk shirt he wore adorned with gold cufflinks. "You could have fooled me."

"She had reservations on a galleon dinner cruise. She was clearly not relishing the thought of attending it alone. I didn't want her to have to miss out on the joy of something like that because of her worthless ex-fiancé's actions."

Leo studied him a beat. "And?"

"And that's the only reason we were out together."

"Right. So you asked her out on a date. You just lucked out that it was already paid for. Got it."

That was it. Vito gave up. Why was he even trying? He followed Leo to where the women stood ordering gelatos.

Vito understood that both Lynetta and Leo had good intentions. They wanted him to move on with his life. They wanted for him what they themselves had: a strong union, beautiful children, a happy homelife. For an insane moment, he let himself indulge in just such a fantasy as he watched Maya walking ahead of him. He pictured the two of them putting a couple of rambunctious toddlers to sleep then slipping out to spend some alone time together.

Then he made himself shake the images away. Things like family and a home full of children simply weren't in the cards for him. Marina had told him repeatedly that he didn't have the capability to fully love someone. That he was too consumed with his art, his craft. To the detriment of everything else that was important. He'd denied it right up until the point when he'd proven her right.

When he reached her side, Maya gave him a hesitant look. If things had been awkward between them before, they were downright uncomfortable now.

Maybe she would find a way to wriggle out of the invitation to visit Nonna. It wasn't like she'd have to face Lynetta if she blew them all off. Once she left Venice, she'd never see either of his cousins again.

He wasn't the slightest bit surprised that the notion of her bailing on them sent a bolt of disappointment through his chest.

"Maya mentioned you two had already had tiramisu," Lynette informed them. "So we only got the two cones. We can all share."

Right. Somehow he was supposed to watch Maya lick an ice cream cone then share that same cone with her. His body tightened in response to the image.

"She's…uh…something else," Maya said on a near whisper, handing him the cone.

"It's all yours. And, yes, my cousin's wife is certainly one of a kind."

"Great. Even more calories." He had to look away when she took the first lick. How the hell was he supposed to spend a whole day with her in Verona?

"There'll be more tomorrow. There's never a shortage of food at Nonna's place, even under normal circumstances. Let alone any kind of celebratory event like a birthday."

Maya swallowed the bit of gelato. "So it's real, then? I'll be going to Verona with you."

"That's totally up to you, *cara*. You might have to deal with Lynetta's displeasure, however, if you back out."

She gave an exaggerated shudder. "Why does that prospect frighten me so?" She glanced to where the other couple stood taking turns with their own cone. "They both care deeply for you."

"I suppose that would be one way to describe their heavy-handedness."

Maya looked down toward her toes. "Listen, Vito. I know Lynetta sort of finagled this whole invitation. I will find a way to back out of it and face her wrath if I have to."

"Is that what you want?"

"I guess I'm asking what it is that you want."

Now that was essentially the question, wasn't it? The question he hadn't been able to make himself face. Until now. She was due to leave Venice at the end of the week. After that, he might never lay eyes on her again. The thought was increasingly causing him an unwelcome sensation of pain he didn't want to acknowledge. So he decided to tell her the truth.

"I want very much for you to come with me and my family to Verona, *cara*. I'd be honored if you would join us."

What had she gotten herself into?

Maya plopped down fully clothed on the bed as soon as she'd shut her hotel room door behind her. Vito had walked her over to the lobby, then he had bid her a hasty good-night, stressing that they both needed to rest before the big day tomorrow.

She'd expected to be knee-deep in tissues right now, and wondering about what might have been after having bid a final goodbye to Vito. Instead, she was wondering what she should wear tomorrow and how much she should pack. What exactly did one wear to an Italian grandmother's eighty-fifth birthday?

If someone had told her three days ago she'd be pondering that question, she would have pegged them as delusional. She wasn't sure how to feel about this new development. On the one hand, she was thrilled to be able to spend more time with Vito; the moments spent in his company had been some of the most fun-filled of her days so far. On the other hand, she wasn't sure if her heart could handle it. The longer their goodbye was delayed, the harder it was going to be on her emotions.

She was falling for him. Any outside observer would say she was no doubt rebounding, that it had been way too short a time since meeting Vito to have developed any kind of real feelings for him.

They'd be wrong. She knew the truth. As did her heart.

Meeting Vito had made her realize that she hadn't been in love with Matt so much as she had loved the idea of being in love. The idea of having a husband. A future and a family. One she could finally call her own. Not one she'd been forced into.

Now, in contrast, she could tell that she and Matt had never been right for each other. And they never would be.

Her tablet dinged across the room signaling a text. It was her cousin Zelda.

Maya. If you get this text please check your email. Can't get a hold of you.

Maya cringed at the message. She'd been woefully negligent in letting her family know her whereabouts after the loss of her phone. The truth was, she'd been putting off telling them the truth about Matt. A truth she couldn't put off any longer, however.

With a resigned sigh, she walked over and powered up the tablet then tapped the mail icon.

Sure enough, a slew of new messages sat in her inbox. Most of them from Zelda.

Why haven't you called or emailed? We're all worried about you. Matt still in Boston. Says we should ask you for answers. What's going on?!?!

Her other emails were essentially different versions of the same message. Maya tapped the Reply button and began to type on the screen keyboard.

Zelda, sorry to have worried you and everyone else. The truth is I haven't been completely honest with you. Things aren't exactly going well between Matt and me right now. It's why I traveled here alone for the time being.

She'd barely hit the Send button when Zelda's response popped up on her screen.

I knew it! What did he do? I'll strangle him. Better yet, I'll tell Dad. He'll do worse. You better call me, Maya Papaya. As soon as you can. I mean it!

Maya felt her eyes well up, touched by Zelda's immediate and automatic loyalty in response to her announcement. She and her cousins had had their share of differences and arguments; they'd grown up as sisters, after all. And sisters tended to argue.

But deep down, she knew they would both battle the devil himself for her if they had to. Same with her aunt and uncle.

Despite their loyalty and all their love throughout the years, Maya had never quite been able to feel a sense of true belonging. It was nothing overt that her family did to make her feel that way, it was more in the subtle nuances of family dynamics.

That feeling was probably the reason she'd been too hasty in trying to form a family of her own. Committing to a man who was so blatantly wrong for her.

Maya began replying to Zelda's latest email.

No need for strangulation. Matt and I not right for each other. Please don't say anything to Grandmama. She gave so much so that I could enjoy this trip.

Zelda's second response came as quickly as the first.

I won't say anything to Grandmama Fran. Double pinkie swear. But I can tell there are things you're not telling me. Spill!

Maya had to smile at the reference to the sworn declarations they'd made as children, hooking their little fingers to seal any and all deals. She began to type.

I'll call as soon as I can. I promise. Damaged my phone and still trying to work out use of Italian burner. No need to worry. All is well. Just figuring things out right now. Talk soon. Xoxo

With that, she powered down the tablet and stuck it inside her carry-on bag. As much as she loved Zelda and the rest of her family, she didn't have it in her to continue communicating with anyone right now. Not even via dueling emails.

She felt utterly and completely spent after the day of roller-coaster emotions she'd just spent with Vito. No doubt spending a full day with him tomorrow would prove just as perplexing. Plus, the rest of his family would be there to observe and note every move she made. Would she be able to hide her growing feelings for one of their own?

But there was a bigger question that needed to be addressed. How in the world was she supposed to handle those feelings once this fairy tale inevitably ended?

"You did what?" Vito couldn't believe the nonsense Leo was spouting. They'd just disembarked from the jet at Villafranca Airport and were in the process of entering the spacious van that would take them to the Rameri family estate in Verona. And Leo had waited all this time, through about an hour of travel, to mention that he'd told their *nonna* a colossal lie.

"She would have jumped to the conclusion anyway," he explained now, not even slightly contrite for what he'd done. "You know how she is."

Vito had pulled his cousin to the side as Maya and Lynetta handed their luggage to the waiting driver and wrangled the two toddlers into their car seats in the back of the vehicle.

"Did it even occur to you that this might embarrass Maya?"

Leo gave a careless shrug. "I think she'll go along with it. She seems like a flexible sort."

"But what were you thinking, Leo?" Vito

demanded to know. "Why would you tell Nonna that I've asked Maya to marry me?"

Leo placed a hand on Vito's shoulder. "She's worried about you. She thinks you've been wallowing in your grief too long." Leo paused then to give him a pointed look. Clearly, he thought the same way Nonna did on that particular topic. Finally, he continued. "When I called to tell her you'd be bringing a guest, she automatically jumped to the most hopeful conclusion. I didn't have the heart to correct her. She's not getting any younger, you know. It's just a small fib to make an old woman happy for a few days. On her birthday."

"So we're supposed to act like a newly engaged couple around her, is that what you're suggesting?"

"I think you can pull it off. You were doing a pretty good job of it when Lynetta and I came upon the two of you at San Marco."

Vito wasn't going to justify that with any kind of response.

"And what about afterward? When she calls to check on me in a few days and I have no fiancée to speak of? When the woman in question has traveled to a different country?"

Leo gave his shoulder a squeeze. "Then she will have had a few days of hopefulness, won't she?"

"All based on a lie."

"Is it?"

Vito had to give his head a shake. "What do you mean? Of course it's a lie to say that Maya and I are engaged."

His cousin waved his hand in dismissal, as if Vito was missing the point entirely. "Yes, yes. We both know you're not really engaged."

"So that would be a lie. You have lied to Nonna."

"I told her a small fib. And there's something you're not considering."

"What would that be? Please enlighten me, dear cousin."

"Maya doesn't have to be thousands of miles away in a few days. You can simply ask her not to leave."

Leo didn't give him a chance to respond before turning to join the women in the car, leaving Vito to watch his retreating back.

Had his cousin always been so invested in Vito's personal life? What was possessing him to behave so intrusively lately?

His gaze was drawn to where Maya sat in the car. He would have to find a way to explain to her what Leo had done and the resulting chaos that might ensue as a result. Heaven help him find the words to do so. Now she was playing some kind of peek-a-boo game with his older nephew, who was buckled into his seat. The child was squealing with laughter at her antics.

It appeared Maya Talbot had some kind of effect on all manner of Rameri males.

Vito was exceptionally quiet during the ride from the airport. Maya slid another glance in his direction where he sat next to her in the third row of the passenger van. The children had finally calmed enough to settle down and one of them looked on the verge of falling asleep.

By contrast, Vito looked about as far from relaxed as one about to attend a grand party should be.

Was he having second thoughts about having her here? She ought to have thought this through. His invitation had ultimately seemed sincere enough but she couldn't pretend he hadn't been pushed into it by his cousin's wife. He'd probably considered it overnight and regretted asking her. This was to be a family affair, after all. She certainly wasn't family. She was barely more than an acquaintance.

But his reaction to her last night had said otherwise. Her mind drifted to the kiss they'd shared during their cruise. It seemed a lifetime ago. But she hadn't forgotten the way the touch of his lips against hers had made her insides quiver like gelatin.

As much as she hated to admit it, given what it might say about her decision-making abilities, she couldn't recall Matt's kisses having as dramatic an effect on her. And she'd been ready to marry him.

Was she making a different version of the same mistake? Because something clearly wasn't right, judging by Vito's scowl.

Either one of her cousins would be skeptical if she tried to tell them that she was falling for a man she'd met days ago. They'd tell her she was rebounding, that she couldn't see clearly from the hurt. Her aunt and uncle would agree. Perhaps she'd moved too fast. Maybe the kiss on the ship meant nothing to Vito. She might have read too much into it. It obviously wouldn't be the first time she'd misread a man or his intentions.

The questions rambled around in her brain. Questions she could only guess the answers to. She'd never been in a situation like this before. Then again, she'd never met a man like Vito before.

He was charming and enigmatic, without doubt. But his sadness practically resonated in the air around him.

She shouldn't be foolish enough to think

she could possibly be the one who might be able to take that sadness away, not even temporarily.

Vito spent most of the ride from Verona airport to the villa trying to decide how he might explain to Maya what Leo had done. They were less than a mile from the mansion and he still hadn't quite figured it out.

Well, he had to think of something. He couldn't let her be ambushed without a clue when she first met Nonna. He could guess pretty well what Nonna's reaction would be when they were introduced. She'd probably hug the younger woman within an inch of her life. Then she'd start referring to Maya as her future granddaughter to anyone within earshot. Maya had to be prepared for all of it.

In any case, right now she looked like she was ready to be out of the car. The road was full of curves and bends, the driver not exactly the smoothest operator he'd been driven by. Judging by the greenish hue of her complexion at the moment and the way she kept clasping her hand right below her breastbone, he figured she might have had enough of the car ride.

He turned to her. "Would you mind if we

walked the rest of the way? I'd love to show you the vineyards."

Maya seemed to be taken by surprise but she soon nodded and began to gather her sweater around her. In Italian, Vito instructed the driver to stop so that the two of them could get out.

"Please let Nonna know we will be there shortly. Tell her we wanted to get some air after a long morning of travel and that I wanted show Maya the countryside." He addressed Lynetta with the request, his annoyance with Leo still too close to the surface.

"*Sì*, Vito."

Maya turned to him after the vehicle dropped them off and drove away. "Was my car sickness that obvious?"

"It was. But there's another reason I wanted us to walk together for a bit."

"There is?"

He took her gently by the elbow and they started to stroll on the grassy verge by the side of the road. "I'm afraid there's something you need to know before we greet my grandmother. You may not like it."

Hadn't he said those exact words to her that first day at his studio?

"Wow. That sounds pretty serious," she commented.

There really was no easy way to break it to her. Better to just blurt it out. He inhaled deeply. "See, the thing is, my grandmother is under the impression there's more between us then there really is."

She blinked at him. "I beg your pardon? I don't quite understand."

Vito rubbed a weary hand down his face. How had he found himself in such a messy predicament? It was as if he had no idea what direction his life was headed in at any given moment.

Without giving himself too much time to think, he gave Maya the basic rundown of what Leo had done and why. She appeared a bit shell-shocked once he was done.

Welcome to the club, he wanted to tell her.

They'd reached the sprawling vines that abutted the estate gardens. The aromatic scent of grapes permeated the air. Vito reached for a ripe bunch and held it out to her. She still hadn't said a word about what he'd just told her.

Maya took the fruit from him and popped one of the grapes into her mouth. She seemed to savor the taste as she chewed and swallowed. A sudden unwanted desire to feed her one himself made his palm itch. His gaze fell to her mouth. He could still taste those lips of hers on his own, feel their lush fullness. Vito had to remind himself to focus on the matter at hand.

"So, am I supposed to act as if you and I are betrothed?" she asked.

"I know it's ridiculous. You have to believe I had nothing to do with it."

"Oh, I have no doubt you had nothing to do with any of it, Vito."

He could have sworn her tone held a hint of disappointment when she spoke the words. Which made zero sense. He had to have imagined it.

"I'm not sure how I feel about deceiving an unsuspecting grandmother, to be honest."

"This is the type of untruth that's meant solely to give her some pleasure on a milestone day." Truth be told, he hadn't exactly been looking forward to spending the entire time fielding questions about whether he was ready to move on with his life. Not to mention hearing about all the eligible young granddaughters of her friends that Nonna always wanted him to meet. At the least, it would be a refreshing change to spend some time at his estate with the entire family and not have to duck unwelcome suggestions about all the women his family wanted to introduce him to. Of course, this way he and Maya would have to find ways to answer all sorts of questions about how they'd met and fallen in love.

Surprisingly, he didn't think that would take much effort. They could even stick mostly to the truth.

Still, he had to make sure Maya was completely certain that she was up for what he was proposing. "It's only for the afternoon. I understand if you want no part of it." Heaven knew he couldn't blame her for that. "I'll work something out if you're not comfortable."

"It's okay. I'll do it."

Vito released the breath he didn't realize he'd been holding. "You will?"

She slowly pulled another grape off the bunch she held and ate it before she answered. "Sure. Why not? It's your grandmother's birthday, after all. And I find myself attending without a gift. This one small fib seems harmless enough. If it will make her happy on such a momentous day, then I'm happy to do it."

"Grazie, mia bella," Vito said, planting a small peck of a kiss on her cheek. When he straightened, he couldn't help where his thoughts drifted. For one insane moment, he wished with all his heart that the pretense wasn't even necessary. That it might all somehow be real.

CHAPTER NINE

WHAT HAD SHE just agreed to? To think, when he'd asked her to walk with him, she'd initially thought it was because he wanted to spend time alone with her before the chaos began. As if.

Still, Maya hadn't quite been prepared for what he'd just announced. In fact, she was woefully unprepared for this whole day. How was she supposed to spend the entire time by Vito's side, ignoring the way he affected her? How would she clamp down on the arousal he fanned deep within her core? Now there was the added complication of having to pretend they were lovers.

Not that she hadn't imagined just such a thing. Though, in her imaginings, there hadn't been a need for pretense.

"I suppose we ought to get some sort of basic story in order. At the least, we should be consistent about what we tell everyone.

Lynetta and Leo will have to play along, of course."

"It's probably wise to stick as close to the truth as possible."

"I would agree."

"We could tell them I fell when I first saw you. Quite literally. And you fell in a much more poetic, figurative sense." See, she could be good at this. Not bad for an off-the-cuff suggestion.

Vito chuckled beside her. "I like it, *cara*. Though maybe we should be sparse with the details."

"Like how tipsy I was?"

"More that you had just freed yourself of one fiancé."

What an apt description. She hadn't known it at the time, but Matt had, in fact, freed her. From a mistake that would have followed her for a lifetime. She had to wonder if Matt had simply seen the inevitable: that they both deserved more out of life than what they'd been settling for. She might actually owe Matt a thank-you if one were to truly examine it. That thought would have had her quaking in shock a few short days ago.

"Yes, let's definitely omit that little tidbit," she said as they walked farther along. Once they crested the hill, the house came into full view.

Maya had to do a double take. She wasn't sure what she'd been expecting, but it was certainly a bit more modest than this three-story structure with Ionic columns surrounded by rolling hills.

"That's your grandmother's house?"

"Yes. More accurately, it's the family estate. Leo and Lynetta come here often with the boys. As do I. It's a short enough trip from Venice."

"It's quite the mansion."

"Do you like it?"

What was there not to like? "It looks like something out of a painting. A sprawling house and the lush greenery as the backdrop."

Vito placed both hands on his hips and studied the house in the distance. "Huh, I guess you're right."

She gave him a playful shove on the arm. "You're toying with me. Of course you must have seen it yourself. Accomplished artist that you are."

He shrugged. "I guess I just always viewed it more as home."

Once they drew closer, Maya could see the festive decorations. The house looked every bit ready for a birthday bash. Decorative balloons adorned the windows. Colorful streamers had been wrapped around the columns.

Lively music could be heard coming from somewhere within.

Without warning, a large mound of fur came flying at them from the direction of the house.

"Romeo!" Vito shouted, then he roared with laughter as the ball of fur reached him and jumped up. He spoke affectionately in Italian as he gave the dog a thorough petting.

"This is Romeo," he told her. "He's a very good *mimmo*."

Maya leaned down to greet the dog. He responded with a wet lick on her cheek.

"He likes you," Vito declared. "Juliet should be around here somewhere."

Maya straightened. "You have two dogs that are named Romeo and Juliet?"

He gave her a playful smile. "We are in Verona, after all."

Of course. That made sense.

"There's a surprise twist," Vito added in a mock whisper, cupping his hand against his mouth as he spoke.

"What's that?"

"They're both boys."

"Hmm. That is surprising, indeed. I did not see that coming."

Vito nodded solemnly, rousing a gurgle of laughter from her. "When you meet Juliet,

please do not inform him that he is the name-
sake of one of fiction's most notable hero-
ines."

"Why not?" Maya asked. "For all you
know, he might find it an honor."

Vito rubbed his chin, contemplating this
possibility. "Huh. Never thought of it that
way."

She winked at him and popped another one
of the luscious grapes into her mouth from
the bunch she still carried. It exploded in her
mouth, a mini ball of flavor.

Vito's expression suddenly hardened and
turned serious as he watched her. His eyes
grew dark. *Heaven help me*. She thought she
read desire in their depths.

He stepped toward her, his hand reaching
for her face. Maya's breath caught in her chest
as he rubbed his thumb over her bottom lip.

"Not all of the juice from your last grape
made it into your mouth, *cara*." His voice was
thick and raw.

Maya turned her face into his palm. Trem-
ors ran over the surface of her skin. The
slightest touch from this man had the most
dramatic effect on her. She longed for more;
she wanted him to kiss her once again. Without thinking, she tilted her chin up, ran her
hand along his forearm.

"Mia bella," Vito whispered, so close now that the heat of his breath danced over her cheek. Then she lost any sense of focus whatsoever as his lips touched hers.

A sudden commotion from behind her had her startled and stepping out his grasp. Maya turned to find a rotund older woman emerging from the house then heading in their direction. She had to be Vito's grandmother.

Of course, Maya thought as the older woman approached them with her arms outstretched and a wide grin on her face. Vito must have known his Nonna was watching this whole time.

Their kiss had been nothing more than a show for her sake.

CHAPTER TEN

"I BROUGHT YOU a plate."

Maya looked up to find Lynetta standing before her where she sat on one of the porch rocking chairs. The last hour had gone by in a dizzying haze. She'd been introduced to so many people, and Nonna had kept finding her to affectionately pat her on the cheek at regular intervals. So far, the charade was going off without a hitch. But Maya found herself exhausted and in need of a break.

"I hope I'm not intruding on a private moment," Lynetta added. Maya reached up to help her with her load. In addition to a large tray piled with food, she was carrying two bottles of iced tea. Maya relieved her of the beverages; the tray looked much too precariously balanced to attempt to take it.

"No. You're not. I just needed a quiet moment. You Rameris are a boisterous lot."

Lynetta sat down on the matching rocking

chair next to her and placed the tray on the little table between them.

"This was very nice of you," she told Lynetta, enjoying a long swallow of the iced tea. She hadn't realized how dry her throat had become after holding so many language-challenged conversations.

And now that she was presented with a loaded antipasto tray, her stomach reminded her with a low growl that she was hungry, as well.

"You're welcome. Though you might not be thanking me once dinner is served and you're already full," Lynetta answered with a smile. "It's never a good idea to munch before Nonna's big dinners. But the side table full of artisan cheese, cured meat and pickled olives looked too good to ignore."

"So I see. Did you happen to leave anything on the table for the rest of them?"

Lynetta bit into a crusty piece of bread and Maya followed suit. The morsel tasted fresh out of the oven and practically melted in her mouth.

"Trust me, there's more than enough for every man, woman and child here."

"As well as some aptly named canines?" Maya jokingly asked.

"Yes, them too," Lynetta replied.

"Nothing like massive quantities of Italian food to ensure everyone's happiness."

Lynetta's expression suddenly turned much more serious as she stared at the rows of vines in the distance. "Actually, this is the happiest we've seen Vito in quite some time. The last few years, when we've all gathered for one reason or another, he just appeared to be going through the motions. As if he couldn't wait to get the day over with and return to the dark depths of his studio."

Maya's heart tugged at that depiction. From what Lynetta was saying, Vito hadn't even found comfort and joy surrounded by so many of his loved ones.

"I'm so sorry to hear that. He deserves much more in his life."

Lynetta nodded in agreement. "He certainly does. That's why we're all very happy that he seems to be turning the tide somewhat. Leo swears the change started right when he met you."

Maya's pulse quickened at the implication. "I'm not sure what to say to that, Lynetta," she responded honestly. "Only that Vito maybe needed a temporary diversion in the form of a distracted, clumsy American tourist. One who is set to leave Venice in a few days."

The other woman turned to her with one elegantly shaped dark eyebrow lifted. "You appear to be much more than a mere diversion, Maya."

Maya suddenly found it hard to swallow the small cube of provolone she'd popped into her mouth. What Lynetta thought she saw between Maya and Vito wasn't necessarily real.

She found herself admitting out loud the concern she'd been harboring all this time and had been too chicken to address. "I think the temporary nature of my presence might be what's drawing him, Lynetta." She hated the needy quality that dripped from her voice as she spoke the words, though she felt a profound sense of relief at being able to finally share her fear with an interested party. She took a deep breath and made herself continue. "I think the fact that I'll be leaving in a few days and out of his life after that makes me a safe bet as a distraction." Maya bit back the sob that had lodged itself in the back of her throat.

"Is that what you really think?"

"He hasn't mentioned anything about staying in touch afterward. Aside from promising to mail out the sketch he drew of me that first day, he makes no indication that we'll be in touch at all."

"Have you mentioned doing so?"

Maya looked down at her toes. "I don't want to push a man who isn't ready. Not with what little I can offer."

Lynetta didn't tear her gaze from the rolling hills in the distance. "I see," she offered simply.

Maya felt compelled to continue. It felt good to be able to get this off her chest, to talk to someone who seemed to care about Vito. And who might have a care or two about the new American she'd just met, as well. "He's been through a lot. I know he needs time to grieve. And to heal."

"I don't disagree." Lynetta kicked off her sandals and slowly rocked her chair. "But at some point, he needs to start."

At Maya's silence, the other woman continued. "Until you came along, he hadn't showed any signs of beginning that process."

A bud of pleasure blossomed in her chest at Lynetta's words. It was quickly followed by a profound sense of sadness. Even if everything Lynetta said was the absolute truth, it hardly made a difference. She and Vito had separate lives thousands of miles away from each other.

No matter what was happening between them, they would always be worlds apart.

"Vito takes too much of the blame upon himself," Lynetta stated several moments later after a contemplative silence had settled between the two women. Her comment didn't take Maya by surprise at all. Not after what Vito had said during their time on the galleon. The sounds of laughter and music could be heard echoing from the house behind them. An occasional child's shriek and the bark of a dog punctuated the background noise.

"He alluded as much to me," Maya answered. "But then he seemed uninterested in talking about it further. I didn't want to push."

"Vito never wants to talk about the accident. Not that I can blame him. I do blame him for trying to take full responsibility for it, however. It's dreadfully unfair."

"Is there a reason he does so?"

"He believes there is. Has he told you much about Marina?"

Maya shook her head and took another sip of her drink. "Nothing, really. He must have loved her very much."

"Mmm-hmm. They were both very much in love." She paused briefly. "In the beginning."

The pause was not lost on Maya. "Did something happen?"

"Yes. And no."

Well, that certainly clears it up, Maya thought sarcastically. She waited for Lynetta to elaborate.

"Marina was an...interesting type of woman. So passionate about everything. Sometimes her passion was too much for one man to deal with. Even a man as capable and as willing as Vito."

Maya was trying desperately not to take the things Lynetta was telling her to heart. It was difficult to sit there and listen to someone talk about Vito's love and life with a different woman. A woman he clearly still pined for.

"When they first met, Vito created some beautiful sculptures. Even more noteworthy than what he'd done before. His career was already on its way. But suddenly it took off. She truly inspired him."

So, he'd lost his muse as well as his wife. Was it any wonder he was having trouble moving on? Not that it was any kind of competition, especially considering the poor woman had passed in such a tragic manner. But if it were, how could Maya possibly compete with someone who'd shared Vito's bed *and* provided him with creative impetus?

Lynetta continued. "But Vito is a true creative. He was constantly growing. Constantly expanding the scope of his work. Eventually,

Marina became less of a factor in his creations. That's when the trouble began."

"Trouble?"

It hadn't occurred to Maya that Vito and his wife had been anything less than blissfully happy. Why else would he be so hard on himself about losing her? She didn't know the details and couldn't bring herself to ask him. But she'd assumed that he was plagued with guilt about not being able to protect the woman he loved.

"He never spoke to us about any of it. He would never have betrayed her privacy that way." Lynetta stopped her rocking. "But we witnessed enough of the arguments firsthand. And the way she lashed out after each one."

"She…lashed out?"

"Oh, yes. In phenomenally dramatic fashion. Sometimes in public. Several times in front of Vito's family and friends."

Maya didn't want to think about what that would have done to a man like Vito. He seemed so private, so proud. Having witnesses to the failings of his marriage must have been a terribly difficult burden. No one should be subjected to such a public display of their relationship troubles.

Maya shuddered at the prospect. She dreaded the moment when she had to finally

confide to her family about her breakup with
Matt. Bad enough that she would have to tell
them about it. She didn't want to think about
how it would feel to have had them witness
it firsthand.

"Nothing Vito did was enough," Lynetta
went on. "Marina wanted his complete attention. When she didn't get it…"

Lynetta didn't finish her sentence. Suddenly, she performed the sign of the cross
and closed her eyes tightly. Maya could hear
the quick prayer she uttered in Italian.

"Forgive me for speaking ill of the de-
ceased," Lynetta said, opening her eyes again.
"I just felt you should know the basic facts
about Vito's past. It's only fair to you, given
how close you and Vito have become in such
a short time."

The questions rambled through Maya's
brain. What had led to Marina's fatal accident? Why exactly did Vito think he was directly to blame for it?

Would he ever trust her enough to confide
in her about any of it?

Lynetta stood then, lifted the tray of half-
eaten food and walked to the front door. "I
should go check on the boys. Excuse me."

But Maya had so many other questions;
Lynetta couldn't just leave after all she'd re-

vealed. "Lynetta, wait. Please, I'd just like to know—"

But the other woman didn't let her finish. "I'm sorry. I really am. But I've said more than enough. The rest he will have to tell you himself."

"There you are."

Maya wasn't sure how long she'd sat there after Lynetta left. When Vito found her, she was still deep in thought and dusk had settled across the horizon.

"I was just admiring the view."

"If you think that view is special, wait until you see what's in store next." He held out a hand to her. "Come on. Let's go."

"Where are we going?"

He'd already taken her wrist and pulled her up. They walked to the side of the house and down the porch steps. Parked around the corner were three golf carts.

"You still haven't told me where we're going," she reminded Vito as he led her to one of the carts and had her climb in. Leo and Lynetta noisily burst through the side door and commandeered the cart behind them. They were followed by two other couples she'd been introduced to upon arrival though she couldn't quite recall any names.

Soon they were driving past the house and into the fields.

"Am I the only one who doesn't know what's going on?"

"You'll see, *cara*. I think you'll like it."

Maya studied his profile as he drove. His hair ruffled in the wind as he picked up speed. A deep smile creased his lips. He had his shirtsleeves rolled up and the top buttons of his shirt undone. The man could carry off any look, like a male magazine cover model. He was just as strikingly handsome dressed in a casual shirt and khakis as he had been in a tailored tuxedo.

She recalled Lynetta's words. In all fairness to Marina, she could see how a man like him would elicit strong and passionate emotions from the woman he loved. But what Lynetta had described sounded toxic.

Maya didn't get a chance to further explore that thought. When they cleared a large hill, she got a glimpse of what all the activity was about. In front of them sat three large hot air balloons.

Maya couldn't hold back her shriek of delight. "Oh, my!"

"Surprised?"

"Thrilled!"

A bolt of excitement shot down her spine.

Vito came to a stop about a yard away from the balloons. Seconds later, Leo parked next to them.

Maya jumped out of the cart and took in the sight of the towering, colorful balloons. She'd never been in one before. To have her first ride happen in Italy was almost too good to be true. To think, in a few short moments, she'd be gliding through the air over some of Europe's most majestic sights.

And Vito would be by her side.

She couldn't help it. The excitement was too much. She turned and threw her arms around his neck. His reaction was immediate. His hands gripped her waist and he pulled her closer. Then he dropped a small kiss on her lips.

"I like knowing I've pleased you," he whispered against her ear, his breath hot against her cheek.

Good thing he was holding on to her. Her knees almost buckled.

"Let's go, you two." Leo's voice sounded from behind them. "You can do all your embracing after we ride." Lynetta was hard on her husband's heels. She seemed at least as excited as Maya.

"Shall we go, then?" Vito asked but made no move to release her.

Maya reluctantly pulled herself out of Vito's arms. He kept his hand at the small of her back as he led her to the balloon in the middle. The pilot greeted them with a wide smile and helped her in.

Within moments, they'd lifted off. The breath left her lungs as they rose higher and higher. The thrill of it was exhilarating. She realized she was laughing out loud with delight.

Once they reached altitude, Vito came to stand behind her. He wrapped his arms around her middle, her back snug up against his chest.

"I don't have the words to describe what I'm feeling right now," she said over the noise of the burner that heated the air inside the balloon. To think, she'd almost spent the day back at her hotel, wallowing alone and missing Vito with all her being.

A small voice nagged at the back of her mind that Leo had been the one to initiate her presence here. Not Vito. She pushed the thought aside. All that mattered was that she was here. With Vito holding her as she enjoyed the experience of a lifetime.

In the distance, they could see the river Adige meandering through the city and out into the countryside.

"Turns out it's the perfect evening for it, *sì*?"

"*Sì*, Vito. Everything about this day is perfect."

He responded with another soft kiss, this one to the side of her cheek. Maya reveled in the sensation of having him so close to her, the way his lips touched her skin. The thrill of being up this high combined with the effect Vito had on her was wreaking havoc on her senses.

"I'm not sure what we would have done if you'd been afraid of heights, *cara*."

She laughed in his arms. "Are you kidding? Do you know the number of times I visit the top of the Prudential building in any given year? My uncle does a lot of work in highrise buildings."

"That's good, I wouldn't have been able to bear leaving you behind."

"You'd have gone without me?" she asked, teasing him.

"Never."

Again, Maya made herself ignore the fact that his original intention had been to be here without her. To experience this ride by himself while she sat alone in a lonely hotel room in Venice. She swatted away the useless, wayward thought like an annoying pest. Right now, all she wanted to do was enjoy herself and take all this in.

The buildings and bridges throughout the city made for quite the view below them in the distance. Grand churches and stone buildings lined the river. The weather was cooperating beautifully. Not a cloud could be seen in the early evening sky.

Maya knew the image before her would be seared into her memory for all time. "I know I've said this often on this trip, but I really do feel as if I'm living inside a large painting at this moment. Like I've somehow stepped into a magnificent work of art that has just happened to miraculously come to life."

She tilted her head slightly to look up at him. "Why don't you paint it?"

He rested his chin atop her shoulder. "I'm a sculptor, *cara*. That sketch I drew of you is the closest I've come to creating a painting. Painting is not my craft."

She shrugged. "So, don't do it for your craft." She snuggled tighter against his length and continued to enjoy the view. As well as the feel of Vito's heat against her back. "Do it for fun. Because doing so calls to you."

Vito didn't respond to her suggestion. He just pulled her tighter against him.

* * *

Vito tried to imagine how much different this day would have been without Maya by his side. Rather than thoroughly enjoying it, as he had, he'd have been counting down the minutes until it was over. He might have even skipped out on the hot air balloon ride altogether.

So what did that mean about the reality of his days after she left?

He wasn't sure if he was ready for the answer. He watched her now as she exited the balloon in front of him. Her skin was flushed, the fabric of her summer dress clinging to all her glorious curves.

Pure temptation.

They'd landed moments ago and were waiting for their ride back to the villa. Vito wasn't sure where they'd landed exactly; he didn't recognize the spot.

The pilot spoke into his phone and informed them that their transportation would arrive shortly. Then the man went to work on his balloon.

It appeared Vito and Maya would have some time to themselves. The other balloons had drifted in different directions throughout the flight.

"Come. Let's sit while we wait." He led her to a tall, lush tree and helped her sit at its base. Then he joined her. Without a word or any kind of preamble, he gathered her into his arms and partly on his lap, with his back up against the tree trunk. She didn't argue or resist.

When had this happened? This ease and familiar level of comfort he felt with her. She belonged here, in his arms. They both seemed to know it.

"I can't wait to tell Zelda and Lexie about my hot air balloon adventure."

He nuzzled his face into the soft texture of her hair; she smelled of roses and fresh fruit. And outdoor Italian air.

"What else will you tell them about, *cara*?" he asked.

She shifted closer into him. Vito cursed internally. His body was reacting to her closeness in ways that weren't exactly convenient at the moment.

"Well, I would tell them I met a hot, charming Italian who swept me off my feet, but I doubt they'd believe me."

"Why not?"

"Because it's too much like a fairy tale I might have dreamed up. Almost as if you're too good to be true. They would no doubt think I've made up an imaginary man in order to make them jealous."

"They'll just have to travel to Italy. To see for themselves."

"Or you could travel to the States."

Vito trailed his knuckles down the soft, smooth skin of her arm.

"Would you consider that, Vito? Traveling to the States?"

Given that the question was a hypothetical one, he wasn't quite sure how to answer. He could lie and tell her that he'd consider it.

No, he wouldn't consider traveling to North America. Not even at the bidding of the desirable woman he held in his arms. For it would be a waste of her time. He had nothing to offer her. No more of himself to give. Vito wouldn't lie to her. He couldn't pretend he was fit to be any kind of man that a woman like Maya deserved.

So he decided on the truth. "I have no plans to travel to America in the future, *cara*. I'm content to stay here where I am."

Maya sat up and shifted to her knees, facing him directly. "Are you, though, Vito? Are you actually content, like you say?"

He felt himself bristle in surprise. Where was this coming from?

"Please, tell me honestly," she continued, her voice pleading. "Lynetta and I were speaking earlier and—"

But he'd heard enough. He stood without giving her a chance to continue. Judging by the direction of her questions, he could guess what she and his cousin-in-law had been speaking of. His failed marriage. And the tragedy that had ensued after it had come crashing down around him.

Neither of them had the right.

"You and Lynetta were talking about me? About my marriage?"

She blinked up at him. "Clearly that bothers you. Why?"

Why? She needed to ask? Wasn't it obvious? He wasn't some torrid subject to be hashed over by one of his relatives and a woman he'd just met and would most likely never see again once the week ended.

He ignored the question. If she didn't know the answer, he didn't have it in him to explain.

He'd been a fool. He'd let himself get careless when it came to Maya. He should have heeded the warning cries that had tried to stop him from walking her to the piazza that day. He should never have accompanied her on the tour. And he certainly shouldn't have had dinner with her that night on the cruise.

He'd let himself indulge in a fantasy because he knew it was all so temporary. He'd allowed himself to forget that he had no business caring about the loneliness of a jilted American as she pursued her newfound goal of being more adventurous. He shouldn't have cared whether she felt awkward and alone at dinner by herself on an intimate cruise meant for two. None of that should have moved him in any way. He'd let his guard down and it had only opened up old wounds he'd fought much too hard and waited way too long to heal. He should have known better.

"I hear the truck approaching. Our ride will be here any minute," he said, without meeting her gaze. He lowered his hand to help her up. She stood without taking it.

What had she said?

Maya sat staring at the moving scenery outside the window of the SUV that was driving them back to Vito's villa. Vito sat unmoving in the seat next to her. Neither of them had spoken a word to the other after being picked up.

She couldn't decide if she was hurt or angry. Both. Now that she thought about it, she could say she felt both. Vito had been beyond offended that Lynetta had spoken to her about him. Clearly, he didn't feel Maya warranted any knowledge of his past.

Not even after the days they'd spent together. Not even after the way he'd held her and caressed her during the balloon ride.

And not even after the way he'd kissed her the night of the dinner cruise.

Her breath hitched in her throat when she recalled the indignation and anger in his eyes while they'd been waiting. He might as well have come out and told her that Vito Rameri was none of her business. That he was no concern of hers.

He was right, of course. She'd been foolish to ever think otherwise and should have known better. Unbelievably, this felt worse than Matt's betrayal, which made no sense whatsoever. She'd been ready to marry him, for heaven's sake.

Despite the magic of the past few hours, she suddenly wished she hadn't come to Verona with him. Because now she had to mingle with all these people, all these strangers she didn't know, and she had to pretend everything was right with her. That she was a woman in love.

Laughable, really. Considering how she now realized that the man seated next to her was little more than a stranger.

CHAPTER ELEVEN

HER RACING PULSE hadn't slowed any by the time their car pulled up beside the wide wraparound porch she'd left only a couple of hours ago.

Vito's grandmother stepped out the front door to wave them in. "You're finally back," she declared in a thick Italian accent that served to make her even more endearing. "Come. Dinner is served. Eat."

The elderly lady seemed so happy to see them. As upset as she was, Maya didn't want her sour mood to mar the day whatsoever for anyone else. Particularly not the matriarch that they'd all gathered here to celebrate. Maya resolved to make sure no one enjoyed this day any less due to her presence.

That included Vito.

She waited until his grandmother went back in and laid her hand on his forearm. "Wait."

The look he gave her was loaded with impatience. "What is it?"

Maya took a steadying breath. He wasn't making this apology any easier. Nevertheless, she started giving him one. "I'm sorry if I've overstepped. Lynetta and I were chatting and the subject shifted, not surprisingly, to you. You're the reason I'm here, after all."

"I don't like being the subject of speculation."

"I understand that. I'll be sure to MYOB from now on."

"MYOB?"

"It's an acronym we Americans use. It stands for Mind Your Own Business."

He was about to respond when his *nonna* stepped back onto the porch. "What are you people still doing out here? Your lasagna is getting cold." She added something in Italian with a wave of her hand in Vito's direction.

He took Maya by the elbow. "Come on. We better go in. We can discuss this later. You don't want to keep an Italian grandmother waiting when food has been served."

She followed him silently back into the house though she wanted to ask what was left to discuss. He'd gotten angry and she'd apologized. Episode over.

Everything was now over.

Lynetta had told her that for Maya to find out anything more about him, Vito would have to tell her himself. Clearly, that wouldn't be happening. If she was disappointed or hurt by that fact, she had only herself to blame.

When they made it inside, everyone was already seated around the table and had started serving. One of the toddlers seemed to be wearing marinara sauce all over his face. Numerous Rameris motioned for them to come in and sit.

"What took you so long, cousin?" Leo wanted to know. "Wanted to be alone for a while?"

Vito gave him a look that would have flattened most men where they sat. Leo just laughed in response. Lynetta glanced in Maya's direction, an eyebrow raised in question. Maya gave her a small shrug.

Conversation roared around them, most of it in Italian. Maya took a small bite of the gigantic piece of lasagna that had been set on a plate before her. The smell of garlic and spices tickled her nose. As delicious as it was, and as hungry as she was, she couldn't fully focus on the feast. Vito sat in the chair right next to her, throwing loaded sideways looks at her.

It didn't help that with so many people seated at the table, their legs kept brushing. Each time she felt the contact, she remembered how it had felt to be held in his arms.

How his lips had felt on her. Something she was not likely to feel again.

Suddenly, Nonna slapped her palm against the table where she sat at the very end. It wasn't a hard smack but it was loud enough that it got everyone's attention.

"English, everyone," she ordered once all eyes were on her. "Let's not be rude to our American guest."

Maya had never necessarily been shy, but it was a little daunting to have everyone's focus suddenly lasered in on her where she sat. "Oh, that's all right. Please don't inconvenience yourselves. I don't need to understand everything that's being said."

Nonna shook her head. "Nonsense, dear. Of course you do. You're one of us." She clapped her hands in front of her chest. "Vito will have to teach you the language soon, however. Not everyone you'll have at your wedding will be fluent. Tell us what plans you two have made already."

Maya's jaw dropped. Sure, she'd agreed to the pretense of a false engagement. But she hadn't actually expected to be speaking about any kind of wedding. And she certainly hadn't been expecting to do so in front of close to two dozen people.

Her mouth went dry as she tried to come up

with something to say. She suddenly felt Vito's hand on hers; he gave it a reassuring press.

He cleared his throat, sat upright. "Nonna, there's something I need to tell you."

Oh, no. Not like this. Maya willed him to read her mind. His intention was clear. He was going to come clean. Probably to try and spare her from this tortuous situation. She couldn't let him do that. It would ruin everyone's dinner. Not to mention the scrutiny Vito would have to deal with afterward. She gave his knee a gentle squeeze below the table and shot him a subtle wink. Her silent plea somehow worked. Vito got the hint and sat back in his chair. He gave her a small nod.

"This is all still pretty new, Signora Rameri—"

The older woman interrupted her. "I told you to call me Nonna, dear."

Maya cleared her throat. "Yes… Nonna… what I mean to say is, we're still getting used to being together."

None of that was a lie.

Vito cleared his throat. "That's right. I haven't even got around to getting a ring."

Again, not quite a lie.

"I'm afraid our newfound relationship has caught us both somewhat by surprise," Vito added. He may have been addressing the whole table, but Maya noticed he didn't take his eyes off her as he spoke the words.

It was hours later by the time the dishes had been cleared, rich cannoli had been served for dessert and everyone was getting ready to retire. Vito had given her a small peck on the cheek in view of his grandmother and bid her good-night. Lynetta then showed her to a guest room.

Maya uttered a silent prayer of thanks that no one had had the bright idea to try and put her and Vito in the same quarters. Spending the night alone with him in bed would be more than her emotions could handle right now. She didn't trust herself not to ask for what she so badly wanted.

He was determined to hold back from her, didn't want to share any part of himself. But she couldn't be certain that she wouldn't settle for what she could get if she found herself alone with the man.

She'd just finished brushing her teeth and had slipped on her nightdress when a knock sounded on the door. It had to be Nonna making the rounds to wish her guests good-night. Maya walked over to the door and flung it open, ready to thank the woman for all her hospitality.

She came up short as the words died on her lips. Vito stood in the doorway, an arm casually braced against the wooden frame. When he saw her, his eyes grew dark and traveled down the length of her body.

Maya resisted the urge to cross her arms in front of her chest. Her nightgown was a strappy silk number that she hadn't thought was particularly sexy. But the way Vito stared at her now had her wondering.

"Vito?"

"*Sì, cara.* Sorry to disturb you."

"I…uh…was just getting ready for bed."

"I must say I like the way you slumber."

He didn't look so bad himself. He'd undone yet another button on his shirt, revealing a V of golden tan. His hair had grown more disheveled after the long day they'd had. A wayward curl rested over his forehead, lending him the look of a man with mischief on his mind.

For all she knew, that was an accurate description. Then she remembered the way they'd left things between them. How cross he'd been. Simply because she and Lynetta had discussed his marriage. Clearly, it was a sacred subject as far as he was concerned.

So why was he here at her door right now?

"Do you have a minute, *cara*? There's

something I'd like to show you. It shouldn't take long."

"Uh, sure. I just want to grab something decent to wear."

He said something under his breath. Maya could have sworn he said, "That's too bad."

He was waiting patiently outside her door when Maya returned after grabbing the light cotton sweater she'd packed.

"What is it that I'm to see?"

He motioned for her to follow. He led her down the hall to another doorway. But it wasn't a different room they stepped into. Maya found herself outside on a high balcony overlooking the vineyards and rolling hills. She realized right away what Vito wanted to show her. It wasn't the land.

"Oh, my," was all she could muster. The sky above was the color of deep blue velvet. Stars dotted the darkness and sparkled like the finest diamonds.

Another stunning visual she was not likely to soon forget. Why had she not visited Italy before this? Maybe she might have met Vito if she had. Maybe they would have had a chance to get to know each other before he was married. Before they'd become two people who were so wrong for each other. Before it was all too late for the two of them.

"You should see it during a meteor shower."

If only she could. Maya ignored the sorrow that filled her heart at the thought that she'd never be able to do such a thing. She'd probably never set foot on this balcony again after tonight.

"Can we stay here awhile?" she asked, any hint of tiredness suddenly evaporating.

"Of course." He motioned to the outdoor patio love seat behind them. "Make yourself comfortable."

Maya did so and tucked her legs beneath her on the comfortable cushion. Vito joined her and draped his arm over the back of the couch. A comfortable silence followed, both of them focused on the dazzling view above. She couldn't guess how long they sat there, simply gazing up at the night sky, before Vito finally spoke.

"You handled yourself admirably at dinner. Consider me impressed."

"I didn't want your grandmother's birthday ruined."

"No one but Leo would be to blame if that had happened."

She couldn't argue with him there. Whatever the other man's motivations had been, Leo had to know the truth was bound to come out sooner or later. Not that she'd be around to witness the fallout.

What would Vito tell Nonna the next time he visited with no fiancée in tow? Would he confess it had all been a ruse? Maybe he'd make up a story about their unexpected and terribly sad breakup.

Again, she wouldn't be around so it really was none of her concern. But she couldn't help but want to know. Maybe he'd call her in Boston. They could have a chat about it over the phone. Like casual long-distance friends who kept in touch once in a while.

She had to bite back a sob.

Vito interrupted her speculations with his next comment. "I'd like to apologize for the way I reacted after the balloon ride today. When I learned about the conversation you had with Lynetta."

She hadn't seen that coming. "Why did it bother you so much, Vito? That we'd discussed you."

His profile made for a stark silhouette in the darkness. He exhaled deeply before he answered. "Because it most likely meant you discussed my marriage. My marriage is not something I like people to dwell on."

She'd guessed correctly on that score. "Fair enough." She would let the matter drop. Despite her burning curiosity, she would respect his wishes.

To her surprise, Vito was the one who continued with the topic.

He bent over and leaned both elbows on his knees. "My wife was a woman with strong emotions. I thought I was up for the challenges that came with such a characteristic. I was wrong. I didn't handle it very well."

She reached for him, rubbed a hand over his shoulder in comfort. "You can tell me, Vito. Only as much as you like."

He was silent so long that Maya thought he wasn't going to do any such thing. His voice was strained and gravelly when he finally did speak. "Marina was used to being the center of attention. When we first met, I was happy to give her all of mine. I even based some of my creations on inspiration she provided. But that didn't last. It couldn't."

That wasn't a burden that a healthy relationship could survive, Maya thought. But she remained silent, letting Vito get all that he wanted to off his chest.

"As you can guess, things went sour quickly. I convinced myself none of it was my fault. I told myself I couldn't be expected to be all that she wanted, that she needed. I had my career. My name recognition and accolades of my artwork were growing throughout the world. The more in demand my work became, the more miserable Marina grew. She complained I never had time for her. That we never did things together. Even accused me once of being unfaithful."

He sighed before continuing. "She started giving me ultimatums. But I was too busy to pay attention. The perfect cliché of the distracted artist too engrossed in his work to realize what was happening right under his nose."

"What happened?"

"Marina was growing more and more resentful. Depressed. She said she'd make me sorry for tossing her aside like a useless doll. For the life of me, I didn't think she'd take things that far."

No wonder the man behaved like he carried the weight of the world on his shoulders.

"The more she threatened, the less I listened. I thought she meant she was getting ready to leave me." Vito rubbed his eyes. She couldn't be sure in the dark, but she thought she saw his hand shaking. "I'm ashamed to say that didn't bother me as much as it should have. I felt maybe a divorce wouldn't be such a bad idea, given how bad things had become."

"But that wasn't what she meant, was it?"

"That's just it, *cara*. I don't know for certain. I'll never know what she meant."

"I don't understand."

"She stormed out one afternoon, said she was heading to visit her parents on the Amalfi Coast. I didn't hear from her for a whole week." He sucked in a deep breath. "And I never bothered to call and check on her."

"Oh, Vito." Maya felt the sting of tears in her eyes; the anguish pouring from Vito was nearly tangible.

"I got a phone call late one night that she'd lost control of her car while driving along the cliffs in Sorrento. I hadn't so much as spoken to her in days."

Maya wanted desperately to comfort him, to find a way to console him. But she knew there weren't any words to address what he was going through and the guilt he still dealt with even after more than three years.

Nothing she could say would make a difference. Not only did Vito have to contend with his wife's death, it appeared he would always question whether or not it had indeed been an accident.

And if he had indirectly been the cause of it all.

CHAPTER TWELVE

"You didn't have to walk me back to the hotel," Maya said softly as they reached the entrance.

Vito had spent most of the trip back from Verona trying to determine exactly what he would say to her once they reached Venice. He found himself still at a loss for words now that they'd arrived. He reached over to tug a wayward strand of hair that had fallen over Maya's cheek before he answered. "What kind of gentleman would I be if I left you to see yourself home?"

"I'm not sure how to answer that." She bit her bottom lip and shifted from one foot to the other. There was something on her mind. Something she was debating whether or not to voice out loud. "I'm also not sure if I should invite you upstairs."

There it was. He'd been wondering how this particular goodbye would play out. "Would you like to?"

"Me wanting to do something doesn't always mean it's a good idea."

"If you were ready to do so, it wouldn't be such an agonizing decision." He wouldn't push her. The decision was hers and hers alone to make. He knew she only had one more day in Venice. Then she was off to Florence. And making her way farther out of his life. One step at a time.

A weight settled in the area of his chest at that thought. But he knew it was for the best. She needed to move on with her life. Her days in his city were nothing more than a fun getaway for her. A nice little vacation that happened to come at a time of a major upheaval in her life. No doubt the hurt she was nursing from the scoundrel who'd betrayed her was clouding her judgment. She hadn't even had time to really process the breakup. Now that her visit to Venice was ending, Vito needed to give her the time to do just that. He had no choice but to watch her walk away. They'd both known whatever they'd enjoyed together was to be finite.

"I know I've said it before, but your ex-fiancé is a fool, *cara*."

She blinked up at him, a wealth of emotion behind her eyes. "You can't say things like that, Vito. Not when you're standing here trying to figure out a way to say goodbye to me. Forever."

"That's not what I'm doing."

"Isn't it?" She blew out a deep breath and looked away, off to the side.

"You still have one more day in Venice, do you not?"

She nodded slowly.

"You know where to find me, *cara*. Come by the studio tomorrow if you'd like." He hadn't known he was going to say the words until they'd actually left his mouth. But he found he simply wasn't ready to have it all end so suddenly. Not when she had a few more hours. He would take any of that time she was willing to give him. But it had to be her choice, and hers alone. "It will be your decision whether this is to be our goodbye or not."

She didn't answer before she turned and entered the lobby.

She should spend the day packing and finally catching up on her missed emails and texts. Then she should indulge in one last walking tour around this beautiful city. After all, Maya didn't know when, or even if, she'd ever be back. Despite spending some of the most momentous days of her life here.

What she absolutely should not do was take Vito up on his offer to see him once more.

Maya walked over to the small bathroom in her hotel suite and turned the shower on. As the steaming hot water washed over her, she decided that she'd made the right decision. A clean break would be easiest. Better to just rip off the bandage. Only sometimes ripping said bandage off too quickly resulted in losing a bit of skin. Sometimes it resulted in a wound that left a lasting scar.

By the time she'd toweled off, Maya knew she'd been fooling herself. Who was she kidding? Of course she was going to go see him. There was no way they could leave things between them as it all stood now. Her mind might be trying to tell her one thing, but her heart had other plans.

In the end, her heart won out. She found herself pushing through the door of Vito's studio an hour later.

He immediately stood up from behind the marble counter. "You came, *cara*. I wasn't sure that you would."

Well, she hadn't been, either. Right up until she'd found herself at his door. "I actually turned around twice to go back."

Looking at him now, she was so very glad she'd trudged on. He looked like he hadn't slept a wink since leaving her side. Dark circles framed his eyes and his hair looked as if he'd been ramming his fingers through it all night.

Was it possible he'd been thinking of her as often as she'd thought of him?

"What made you change your mind?" he wanted to know.

"Which time?"

Vito chuckled and stepped closer. She could smell that distinctive scent of his that had somehow grown familiar in such a short time. He trailed a finger along her jawline up to her temple. The simple touch sent a fiery surge of longing through her center.

How could she have thought she'd been in love with Matt? She'd been so naive.

"We'll have to find a way to celebrate your final day in Venice," Vito said softly, leaning in so close, she thought he might kiss her. He didn't.

He took her by the hand. "I want to show you something."

Maya followed him to the back room where she'd fallen asleep just a few days ago. He led her to the easel in the center of the room.

A painting. It was in its earliest stages. But she could see clearly what he intended it to be: the view of the Verona countryside from high above. The view they'd watched together in the hot air balloon. The way he'd captured the images, the sunlight as it fell on the countryside, the sheer detail—it was nothing less than breathtaking.

"Oh, Vito. It's lovely," she murmured, though the word fell far short.

"You're the reason it exists. I was up all night working on it."

"I don't know what to say."

"Don't say anything, *cara*. But to tell you the truth, as much as I enjoyed painting what I have so far, I'd like to put this project aside. For now, anyway."

"You would? But why?"

"There's something else I'd like to begin painting. Some*one*, to be more specific."

"There is?"

"Yes. You. If you'll allow it, I'd like to paint a portrait of you."

Maya bit back her cry of surprise. This was not how she'd expected their final day together to begin. She'd tossed and turned all night; images of Vito and the time they'd shared haunted her dreams if she so much as closed her eyes. It looked like he'd been thinking of her, too. Only in an entirely different way.

She wasn't sure quite what to make of that.

"You want to paint me?"

He nodded. *"Sì."*

"Like one of your French girls?" It was a bad joke, and one he didn't seem to get.

"I beg your pardon? What French girls?"

"You know, from the movie?"

Vito continued staring at her with a blank look.

"You have to know it. It was a huge block-buster. In fact, there's a famous Italian actor who stars in it."

He shook his head. "I don't watch too many movies."

"Never mind."

"So what do you say, *cara*? Are you ready to be my subject?"

Maya thought once more about how differently this day was playing out than anything she could have imagined. The man before her seemed to have entered her life only to throw one curveball at her after another. But, like it or not, she had to admit she'd found that part of his charm.

"What do you want me to do?"

Twenty minutes later, Maya found herself perched atop a high stool in Vito's back room.

Even though he stood several feet away and wasn't so much as touching her, it had to be one of the most intimate experiences she'd ever had with a man. Maya may have been fully clothed, but the way Vito had tousled her hair, the way he'd arranged her flowing skirt to cover only halfway down her thighs and the way he'd pulled her blouse off her shoulder made her feel as if he'd stopped for some reason in the process of undressing his lover. And that's how she felt. As if she were waiting for her lover.

Vito worked silently, the only sound in the room the steady ticking of the clock hanging on the opposite wall.

After what seemed like an eternity had passed, just when she thought she couldn't hold the pose a second longer, he set down his brush on the easel's holding tray.

"We can stop for now. I think I have enough detail to continue on without you having to model."

Maya sighed with relief and kneaded out the kinks in her various muscles. Who knew so many parts of the body could go stiff and tight all at once? When she felt some of the circulation returning to her limbs, she slowly stood and walked over to where Vito was still stroking a brush over the surface of the canvas.

"What do you think?" he asked her when she'd reached his side.

Maya did a double take when she saw what he'd created. She hardly recognized the woman on the canvas.

It took a moment to form the words. "I'm in awe, Vito. What you've created here…"

It was so much more nuanced than the initial sketch he'd drawn of her that first day. Layers of depth that captured her likeness in a way that made her want to become more like the woman he must view her as to be able to paint this portrait.

Maya wasn't sure how to put what she was feeling into words. "This woman you've drawn, she seems so sure of herself. The way she holds her head, the upward tilt of her chin. The steadiness in her eyes. These are all qualities you see in me?"

"Yes," Vito answered simply. "I think the better question is, how do you not see all that in yourself?"

Maya hadn't answered his question. She hadn't spoken much at all since she'd taken a look at his work. By contrast, whenever he'd created anything with Marina in mind, his wife had made all sorts of suggestions and comments. Marina had had no shortage of opinions on his work, whether she'd inspired the piece or not.

But Maya still wasn't saying much. She simply stood staring at the easel, open-mouthed. He had to acknowledge the potential blow to his artistic pride if she actually disliked the painting.

"Is something the matter, *cara*?"

Maya nodded slowly, still silent. In fact, her silence was about to drive him crazy.

"What is it, *bella*?"

"I have a confession to make." She finally spoke, though in barely more than a whisper. "I've been thinking about the way you kissed me the night of the dinner cruise. And how much I'd like you to kiss me again."

Vito couldn't stop himself; he was human, after all. He pulled her toward him and indulged himself the way he'd so badly wanted to since he first laid eyes on her.

But this wasn't the short, light kiss they'd shared the night she was referring to. Vito unleashed all the desire and passion he'd been feeling for her.

She tasted of strawberries and sweet cream. She felt like redemption.

When they finally managed to pull apart, he almost couldn't bear the separation. Her lips were swollen from his kiss, her eyes cloudy with desire. He reached for her again as she spoke.

"I have another confession."

"Yes, *cara*?"

"I'd like more than a kiss, Vito. Much more."

A ball of fire rocketed through his entire body. There was no way he could deny her. Or himself. Though he knew this was oh, so wrong of him. What he was doing was beyond selfish. Perhaps the most selfish thing he'd ever done. Warning bells rang in his head about taking the next step.

He ignored them and lifted Maya in his arms. She felt right in his embrace. Like she belonged there. She belonged with him. He leaned down to give her another long lingering kiss that stole the breath from them both.

Then he carried her upstairs.

Maya didn't have to open her eyes to know that Vito had left the bed. She'd felt his absence, the loss of the warmth of his body next to hers. Her muscles felt languid, spent. In a very good way. She longed to reach for him again, to have him touch and caress her the way he had most of the afternoon.

Where had he gone?

Forcing herself to sit up, she grabbed the sleeveless shirt he'd been wearing when she'd walked in. Her cheeks flushed when she remembered how she'd practically torn it off him earlier. The way his taut skin had felt under her fingers when she'd finally rid him of it. Throwing the shirt on now, she walked out of the bedroom into the kitchen area.

She found Vito at the stove, tossing some pasta into a pot of boiling water. He was shirtless, wearing only a loose pair of gray sweats that shouldn't have been appealing in the least, but somehow made her fingers itch to touch him.

She wasn't going to fight the urge.

"I thought you might be hungry. I certainly am." He didn't turn around as he said the words. Maya walked up behind him and wound her arms around his waist. His spine straightened ever so slightly; the muscles of his stomach and back stiffened under her touch.

Maybe it was simply her imagination. But a nagging voice began sounding in her brain. Then it turned into a loud, ringing alarm. Something was off. Maya released her arms and stepped back.

"I don't have much to offer for food," he threw over his shoulder. "Just some packaged pasta. But there's homemade marinara sauce that Nonna sent back with me after my visit."

Me. My.

Vito may not have even been aware, but

he was using singular terms. Nonna had presented that jar of sauce to both of them when they'd left her home.

It was as if he was mentally erasing her presence in his conversation. Maya's pulse was racing by the time the pasta was done and they were sitting across from each other at the small circular table.

Suddenly, she didn't have much of an appetite.

Vito began piercing the pasta with his fork, so far avoiding all eye contact. Maya knew she wasn't imagining things. She didn't think she could take it if Vito regretted what had just happened between them.

Only one way to find out.

She waited for him to swallow his latest bite. "We need to talk about what just happened between us, Vito."

He didn't bother to stop eating. "I'm not so sure that we do."

"How can you say that?"

"The fact of the matter is that you'll be gone after tomorrow, *cara*. Anything we say to each other will only be empty words. In a few days, we'll be both be back to our normal lives."

He sounded so casual, so nonchalant. Maya wanted to literally cover her ears. But she had to try and get through to him. Or she'd never forgive herself. "I'll be in Europe until the end of the month, Vito. That's a good amount of time."

"To do what?"

What kind of a question was that? She blinked up at him. Was he being deliberately obtuse? "To spend more time together. To try and figure out what we might mean to each other."

"I told you. I have no intention of traveling."

"Not even with me?"

He shook his head. "I'm afraid not."

Each word landed like a sharp spear into her heart. Maya pushed past the hurt and forced her mouth to move. "So that's it, then? And will it be so easy for you to forget all about me after tomorrow?"

"That's not what I said."

"What are you saying, exactly?"

He shrugged. "That I have nothing to give. Nothing to offer."

"That's not true. It's simply the excuse you use to avoid taking any risks."

"But it is the truth, *cara*. I'm not capable of falling in love." He sighed. "I just don't have it in me."

"And what if I've already fallen in love

with you, Vito? What then?" Maya blurted out the words. She had no reason to hide the truth of it now; there was nothing left to lose, after all.

The blood visibly drained from his face. Pushing his plate away, he leaned back in his chair. "I'm sorry, Maya. I can only tell you to try and get past what you think you feel for me. Move ahead with your life as if I don't exist."

A brick settled in her throat. She had to fight to get the words out. "How can you ask me to do that? Do you really think I can?"

He remained silent, and it was answer enough.

"So that's it, then?" she threw out, not bothering to suppress her hurt and anger at his infuriating nonchalance. All the while she was shattering inside. "You've made your decision. And you're basing it all on your grief."

Something visibly shifted behind his eyes. A hardness appeared in his gaze that had her flinching. But she met his stare dead-on. She wasn't about to back down now.

"What is that supposed to mean, exactly?" he asked, his tone gritty and tight.

"I think you know."

"Please indulge me and explain." His voice held a very clear warning. Maya decided she would ignore it.

"I mean that you're so invested in grieving for the past that you refuse to see what the future may hold."

Vito didn't so much as blink. "I see you've decided you can analyze me. Please, tell me more."

She knew he was goading her, that she shouldn't take the bait. But she couldn't seem to help herself. Suddenly, she had too much at stake to stop. She'd never forgive herself if she didn't lay it all on the line. For this man, she had to. "You don't want to move on, Vito. You want to live in the past and examine then reexamine your role in the tragedy that you've had to endure. You don't want to move past it. Because it's easier to dwell on it. Because you're scared."

Vito finally moved. He leaned ever so slightly over the table toward her. "I see. And what about you, *cara*?"

"What about me?"

"What makes you think you've moved on from your past?"

What in the world could he be talking about? He had to see she no longer had any kind of feelings for the man she'd been engaged to. He had to see all her feelings were laser focused on one man and one man alone. "I don't know what you're talking about.

After the afternoon we just shared in your bed, you have to know I've moved past my engagement to another man."

He actually laughed at her. A harsh, mocking sound that echoed off his kitchen ceiling and made her want to shrink away from the noise. "Don't insult my intelligence. I knew it the first time I kissed you on that galleon. I mean the way you've held yourself back your whole life in order to please others."

Her mouth went dry. He had no business speaking of such things. He didn't know her life at all. "Others?"

"Your adoptive family."

"What about them?"

"You've spent your life making sure they never regretted taking you in. From your choice of study in college to your career choice to the man you committed yourself to."

"That's not true. I didn't—" But the words died on her lips. The arguments she wanted to make completely escaped her. It was too hard to think, given the hardness and utter derision in Vito's expression.

"It's exactly what you did," Vito spat out. "You've spent your life making sure you fit in with your adoptive family, molded yourself into what you thought they wanted. Determined to make yourself worthy of their love and acceptance. And you dare accuse me of living for the past."

A cry of anguish tore from her throat before she could stop it. There was nothing more to say, no way she could respond to all the things he'd just said to her. So, he saw her as nothing more than a weakling who'd spent her life trying to appease others. He had no idea. He had no right to make such judgments about her.

She'd been made a fool of. Again by a man. Only this time her heart would never recover.

Maya pushed away from the table on shaky legs. She had to leave before she did something stupid like weep or grovel. She couldn't let him see her do either.

The sooner she got out of there, the sooner she could break down.

CHAPTER THIRTEEN

By the time she checked into her hotel in Florence and went up to her room, close to forty-eight hours later, Maya felt as if an entire lifetime had passed since she'd left Vito's studio. She had a voucher for a late lunch in the hotel restaurant but couldn't summon the will to eat alone yet again. Though it was something she needed to get used to. She'd be spending the rest of this journey by herself.

He could have come with her. Instead, he'd chosen to watch her walk out of his life.

Dropping her bags in the middle of the floor, she willed herself not to cry again. This felt wrong. Totally wrong. A stunning view of the Florence skyline sat before her through her hotel window. She couldn't enjoy it. Instead, she yanked the curtains closed and leaned her forehead against the wall.

This felt worse than the first morning she'd

arrived in Venice, alone and heartbroken over a man she'd thought she'd been in love with.

How mistaken she'd been.

Now that she found herself really and truly in love with Vito Rameri, Maya realized how empty her feelings toward Matt had been in comparison. Matt had never made her insides quiver; he'd never sent desire pulsing through her whole body with a simple smile. He'd never made her want to weep with abandon at the thought that she might never see him again.

Only one man had ever made her feel that way.

And he'd asked her to leave.

The sob she'd been trying to hold in finally escaped. Vito was right. She had to admit it to herself. She'd spent her whole life making sure she never let her immediate family down. Even her decision to get engaged had been made with thoughts of how it would impact her aunt, uncle and cousins.

Maya grabbed the silly burner phone. Calling up the keypad she dialed a familiar Boston number.

But the call didn't connect. Instead, a robotic voice came over the speaker telling her something in Italian. Maya tossed the phone aside and dropped down onto the bed, staring at the ceiling in the dark.

She had no idea what to do next. Her cell phone was useless, she was alone in a strange city and her heart was shattered. What was supposed to have been the trip of a lifetime had turned into nothing more than a source of anguish.

She had no one to blame but herself.

Maya allowed herself a good hour to wallow in sadness and self-pity. Then she sat up and grabbed the hotel phone. Pressing the button for the front desk, she waited.

A friendly female voice answered after the second ring. "*Buongiorno*, Signorina Talbot. How can I assist you?"

"I'd like to make an international call, please."

Zelda's familiar voice came on the line after a series of long beeps.

"Maya Papaya!"

The use of the silly nickname her cousins had tagged her with years ago pulled a smile from Maya's lips. "Hey, Zeezee."

"About time you called. Good timing, too. Lexie is here with the baby."

Longing pulled at Maya's heart. She'd missed them. All of them. Her aunt, uncle, Zelda and Lexie.

She missed the tiny little infant she considered her nephew more than a little cousin. A deep feeling of homesickness rushed through her core, surprising her with its sudden intensity.

"Here, I'll put you on speaker. Say hey to Lexie. And to little Owen."

"Hey, Lex. Hello, little O-man."

"Hi, cuz. We miss you."

"You can't hear it, but he's cooing at you, Maya." The image made her smile even more.

"So, tell us. How is Italy treating you? Were you unable to call until now 'cause you were busy with a hot Roman lover?" Lexie asked, her voice teasing.

Maya bit down on her lip to keep from crying out loud. "Oh…um…"

Zelda immediately read into her response. Or lack thereof.

"Maya? Tell us what's wrong. Is this about Matt? He keeps calling here, you know. Asking how to get a hold of you."

She couldn't bring herself to spare a single thought for Matt right now. He simply wasn't worth it. "No. It's not about Matt." The last word came out with a strained hiccup.

"Sweetie, please talk to me." The genuine concern and affection she heard in Zelda's voice served to finally break the last string of control Maya had been holding on to.

On a shaky breath, she began to tell her cousins the whole complicated story, the words rushing out of her like an overflowing river delta. Beginning with her discovery of Matt's dalliances with a colleague at work and ending with how she'd fallen for a handsome and charming Italian artist who'd turned around and shattered her heart after she'd so willingly and completely given it to him.

When she'd finished, a long silence ensued. For a millisecond, Maya thought maybe the connection had dropped. But then both her cousins started speaking at once. It was impossible to make out the words, though she heard "bastard" thrown about more than once, with a few other choice expressions that would have made Aunt Talley glare in disapproval.

Debatable exactly which man they were referring to.

Finally, the line went silent again.

"Listen to me, Maya." It was Zelda's voice. "Just come home. Come back to Boston."

Maya sniffed and wiped her cheek with the back of her arm. "But Grandmama paid—"

"Grandmama will understand," her cousin

assured her. "She cares more about you than some silly trip she paid for."

Maya couldn't argue with that. When Gran knew all she was dealing with, the woman would waste no time gathering Maya into her arms and consoling her with gallons of tea and mountains of chocolate cake.

"Yes," Lexie added, her voice firm. "Come back here, Maya. As soon as you can."

"Just come home," Zelda repeated. "Come back and let us all take care of you. We'll help you get through this."

Maya couldn't hold back any longer. At the risk of further upsetting her dear cousins, she finally let all the sobs and tears loose. They were right. She had no business traveling through Italy by herself any longer.

She needed to be back in Boston. She needed her family.

Vito's gaze, as well as his focus, kept drifting away from the folded newspaper he had sitting on the table at the outdoor café he frequented. The same café where he'd first laid eyes on Maya Talbot, right before she toppled out of a gondola and fell into his life.

His eye kept wandering to the same spot where he'd first noticed her, as if somehow time might turn back and he'd see her there once more.

She'd said she'd fallen in love with him. And he'd responded by crushing her heart and her spirit.

Vito would have to find a way to live with that knowledge. He'd have to deal with the fact that he'd been a selfish bastard who should never have let things get that far between them. But his callousness had come through yet again.

A shadow suddenly fell over his line of sight. "I thought I'd find you here, cousin."

Leo pulled over a chair from an adjacent table and sat down across from him. Normally, Vito might have groaned with annoyance at the interruption of his solitude by his boisterous, noisy cousin. Today he found he could use the company. Still, he couldn't resist a sarcastic retort. "Please, have a seat, Leo. I'd love it if you'd join me."

Leo reached over and took a sip of Vito's espresso without asking. "You appear to be more mopey than usual. I take it you missed your opportunity to retain something special in your life."

"What's that supposed to mean?"

"You let Maya leave, didn't you? Yesterday was her last day in Venice, yes?"

"Yes. To both questions. And I don't want to talk about it."

Leo signaled to the waiter who gave him a nod. Both men were regulars who didn't need to actually place their drink order.

"Of course you don't want to talk about it. You'd rather not hear me tell you what a fool you can be."

"I presume you're going to tell me anyway. In detail."

Leo rubbed his eyes with the palm of his hand. "Vittorio. Believe me when I say I wish I didn't have to."

"Then don't. I told you, I don't want to discuss Maya. She's gone and will not be returning. The conversation will be moot. Don't waste your breath and my time."

"Fine. Let's talk about you, then."

This time, Vito didn't bother to suppress his groan. Leo ignored it and continued. "How long are you going to beat yourself up about an event that may or may not have happened? An event you weren't the cause of, regardless of how often you try to convince yourself otherwise."

Vito had half a mind to leave the table. But he had no doubt Leo would simply follow him. If they hadn't been out in public, things could very well have turned physical. Vito was all too tempted to head in just such a direction—between the stunt Leo had pulled with the fake engagement at Nonna's and the way he was pressing Vito right now.

He clenched his fist on the table. "I will beat myself up for as long as it takes to come to terms with all that has happened."

"Is that really what you think you're doing? Coming to terms with what happened?"

"Yes, that's exactly what I think," Vito said with finality, hoping against hope that Leo might get the hint and finally drop the subject.

He should have known better.

"Really? Because from where I'm standing, it looks like you're using the past as a reason to hide from the future."

Vito flinched in his seat. The other man's words were nearly identical to the ones Maya had thrown at him. "You go too far, Leo."

But his cousin wasn't ready to back down. He leaned closer over the table between them, bracing his elbows on the glass surface. "You forget I was the one who first saw you after you got that tragic phone call, Vito. I saw the self-loathing you punished yourself with when you had no reason to do so."

The reminder of that night served to temper Vito's anger with Leo. He didn't know what he'd have done if his cousin hadn't shown up to console him moments after Vito had received the news.

"What would you have me do, Leo?"

"Stop punishing yourself," Leo immediately answered.

Vito started to argue. But what would be the point? Leo couldn't understand. Leo had never let his wife down on such an unforgivable level. Lynetta had never felt unloved or ignored. Unlike Vito, his cousin hadn't failed so devastatingly as a spouse.

"Your stubbornness is draining you of all your passion. And all of your will," Leo continued. "You haven't created anything in three years. It's destroying you from inside out to be so dormant. It has to be."

He was wrong about the creating part, Vito mused, thinking of the painting currently sitting on his easel. A painting he'd covered with a drop cloth, unable to bear looking at it now that its subject was gone. Though now he was at a loss as to what to do with it. He died a little inside every time he walked by it. But neither could he bear to throw it away.

"It's not a switch I can flip on and off, Leo."

"Of course not. But you have to have seen over this last week that you can gradually move past your grief. The way you were with Maya reminded me of the man you used to be. Before…" Leo leaned back, not completing his sentence.

He didn't need to. But the man Leo was referring to was gone. Vito had long ago buried him deep within his soul. "I'm not meant for relationships, Leo," he tried to explain. "I learned that the hard way. I can't risk so much again with another woman who might end up paying too steep a price for having loved me."

"Everyone pays a price for love, cousin. You are no exception."

"Nevertheless, I can't give a woman like Maya what she needs. She deserves stability, steadiness. A full commitment from a man to love and cherish her without limits or conditions. I know for a fact that I'm not capable of being that man."

He thought of the way he'd lashed out at her that last day. The look of sheer hurt on her face when his dagger-like words had found their intended targets. What he'd done that day only proved his point: he was unworthy of the love someone like Maya had to give. And incapable of providing all that she deserved.

He slammed his paper down on the table in disgust. This whole conversation was so terribly pointless. "What difference does it make in any case? She's gone. She'll be in Florence by now, then off to the rest of her adventures through Europe."

Leo frowned. "Florence is less than a day's travel." Then he glanced at his watch. "And it's still fairly early."

Vito slowly shook his head. "No. I'm afraid it's too late, Leo. I said some things I can't take back. I doubt very much that she'll forgive me for them." Vito cringed when he thought again of how he'd hurt her in order to ultimately spare her.

"Don't decide that for her, cousin," Leo said. "And it's never too late."

"I'm afraid you're too late, sir. You've just missed Signorina Talbot."

Vito cursed out loud so viciously, the poor young woman at the Grand Hotel Firenze took a startled step back.

He muttered a clipped apology before turning away. Maya was gone. This time for good. She must have altered her plans and left Florence several days early.

Before she returned to Boston, Vito had no way of locating where she was.

He had no choice but to turn around and go back to Venice. Alone.

CHAPTER FOURTEEN

HER AUNT WAS waiting for her at the luggage turnstile at Logan International Airport when Maya deplaned after leaving Florence half a day earlier. A wealth of emotion immediately had tears pooling in Maya's eyes when she saw her. Maya swiped at them before they could fall. She had to resist the urge to run into the older woman's arms and make a spectacle of herself in front of all her fellow travelers.

"Aunt Talley, what are you doing here? I had a car service arranged."

Her aunt gave her a warm smile. "I canceled it, dear. You know you could have asked any one of us to drive you home. Why did you arrange for a car and driver?"

"I didn't want to be a burden."

Her aunt took her by the elbow and walked her to some of the more isolated seats in the arrivals area. "Maybe it's time we had a little talk about that."

"About what?"

"This notion you have that you might be a burden in any way, shape or form to any of us."

Uh-oh. Maya could guess where this was coming from. In her anguish and sorrow when she'd spoken with her cousins over the phone from Florence, she'd overshared all that Vito had said to her. Clearly, word of it all had gotten to her aunt.

As annoyed as she was at her cousins for spilling the proverbial beans, Maya had to concede they'd only had her best interests at heart. She must have sounded like a mess during that call for Zelda and Lexie to have called in the big heavy. As much as Maya loved and respected her uncle, Aunt Talley was the true guiding force behind the Talbot family.

"I was just upset the other day, Aunt Talley," Maya began as they sat down. "I shouldn't have said all that to Zelda and Lexie. I wish they hadn't burdened you with any of it."

Her aunt sighed. "There you go again. Using that word."

"Oops."

"But is it true?"

Maya started to deny it. But Vito's harsh

words echoed in her head. How could she deny that she'd taken up an area of study that she otherwise might not have if her uncle hadn't needed help with his business? Or that she might have pursued a different career with a bigger company after graduation considering how heavily she'd been recruited? Or even whether she would have started dating Matt if her uncle hadn't been so fond of him?

The truth was, she didn't really know anymore how to answer her aunt's question. In so many ways that she hadn't even acknowledged to herself, she supposed she had considered herself something of an unwanted burden upon the family that had taken her in. Subconsciously, she'd been trying most of her life to make sure they never felt that way about her.

"I don't know," she finally answered truthfully. Then she wanted to kick herself at the expression of utter distress on her aunt's face at her response.

"Oh, Maya." Her aunt gently cupped her chin in her hands. "My dear, sweet girl. I will never forgive myself for not reassuring you often and vehemently that you were always a loved and cherished child. Even before your parents were gone, your uncle and I loved you from the moment you were born."

This time, there was no stopping the tears. Maya bit her lip to avoid making a spectacle of herself.

"Forgive me, my dear," her aunt continued, "for not knowing that you might have felt that way for even one minute."

"Please don't say that," Maya pleaded. "I should have known better. I should have come to you."

Aunt Talley gathered her in her arms and held her tight. "Well, allow me to clear the air right now. Uncle Rex and I are both beyond impressed with and fiercely proud of the woman you've become. And we would feel that way no matter what you chose to do with your life. Because we love you, sweetheart. I'm sorry if we didn't say that to you often enough."

Maya couldn't help herself; she leaned into her aunt's embrace and accepted all the love and comfort the woman offered.

It may have been years in the making, but Maya finally felt a warm sense of acceptance and belonging that she'd only been denying herself for far too long.

And she knew she had Vito to thank for it.

Maya jumped in her seat at the booth as Lexie slammed a plastic-coated drinks menu on the table in front of her. "Pick something to order, already," her cousin directed. "We're on our second round."

Maya made a show of opening the menu and pretending to peruse it. What she wanted to drink wasn't available at the popular, trendy Mexican spot that had just opened in Southie. She didn't need to look at it to know that this place didn't carry a rich, fruity Valpolicella like the one she'd been poured the night Vito had kissed her for the first time.

"Hey, come on now." Lexie settled into the seat next to her and nudged her shoulder. "It's been two weeks, Maya Papaya. Try and have some fun tonight."

"I'll try," Maya lied. She was being so unfair and beyond what could be described as a party pooper. This was supposed to be Lexie's first real girls' night out after having the baby and she didn't want to cast a cloud of gloom over her cousin's first outing as a new mom.

"You're still thinking about him, aren't you?"

Maya could only nod. "I'm sorry, Lexie. I should have just stayed home and not risked raining on everyone's good time."

Lexie wagged her finger at her. "We wouldn't have let you. You've been doing enough staying at home since you got back. You go from work to home with a visit to the museum in between. We would have dragged you out if we had to."

Maya leaned her head against her cousin's shoulder. As much as she wanted to, she just couldn't get into the party mood. More than one flirtatious man had tried to approach the table with the four laughing and drinking women. None of those men had even come close to evoking a spark of attraction. She couldn't help but compare them to a dark-haired, charming Italian who'd stolen her heart only to crush it. Each guy had fallen way short in comparison.

"I take it you haven't heard from your man yet?" Lexie wanted to know.

It struck Maya as more than a little funny. She'd been engaged to Matt for close to two years. But every time one of her cousins referred to "her man," they meant the one she'd known for less than two weeks in Italy. A man neither of them had even met.

Not that the term was accurate. "He isn't my man, Lexie. And, no, I haven't heard from him. He hasn't called or emailed. The sketch was delivered but his assistant's name was listed as the sender."

"What about you?" Lexie asked.

"What about me?"

Lexie performed an exaggerated eye roll at the question. "Why haven't you called him?"

Maya straightened in her seat. Calling Vito was out of the question. She'd said what she needed him to know the day he'd sent her away.

"Because he made his feelings very clear," she answered. "I bared my soul and told him I'd fallen in love with him. And do you know what he said?" Maya asked despite the fact that Lexie knew full well the answer to that question. Both of her poor cousins had been made to listen to the whole sordid story almost daily since Maya had landed back at Logan.

Still, Lexie played along. "What did he say?"

"He said that I needed to get past whatever it was I was feeling for him."

"And then what?"

Maya blinked at the query. This was a new line of questioning. Usually Lexie and Zelda simply let her vent and unload everything. Apparently, they'd decided a new approach was in order. "What do you mean?"

"Did you tell him that you didn't want to get past it?"

"Why would I do that?" Maya asked. "What would be the point?"

Lexie shrugged and took a sip of her non-alcoholic beer. "I dunno. I do know you've told us that he's afraid to take a risk, that he was stuck in the past and that's why he let you leave."

"And?"

Lexie reached for her hand over the table and gave it a tight squeeze. "You don't appear to have taken any kind of risk yourself."

"Back again, miss?" The pleasant, smiling young woman on the other side of the window handed her the entrance ticket Maya had just paid for.

Maya returned her smile. "What can I say? I really like the exhibits."

Passing through the turnstile, she walked through the lobby of the Museum of Fine Arts in Boston. Maya had spent every lunch hour here for the past two weeks. She'd splurged on a year-long membership soon after she'd returned to work. Maybe she was being silly, but being here made her feel closer to Vito somehow.

Never mind that he was an ocean away and had probably already forgotten she existed. Well, she would find a way to move on, as well. She had to, didn't she? These museum visits weren't all completely frivolous, either.

Maya had made it a point to check MOFA's website online for openings she might qualify for. She didn't mind starting at a lower position and working her way up. Not that she planned on leaving Uncle Rex's employ all at once. He still needed her. But she needed to make a career change and would do it gradually to eliminate any whiplash effect.

Maya hadn't mentioned the potential job switch to anyone. Not even Grandmama.

She wouldn't do that until she had a few more details solidified. Plus, it didn't help that the person she most wanted to talk to about it was thousands of miles away. Oh, and she couldn't forget that he'd made it more than clear that he didn't really care what her plans for the future held.

Maya had been nothing more than a fling.

Shaking off thoughts of her fateful Venetian trip, she walked over to her favorite gallery, the one featuring Italian paintings. Each time she looked at the masterpieces on the wall, she noticed another detail or learned something new. Each afternoon spent here was never like the one before.

Plus, if she closed her eyes and tried hard enough, she could almost pretend she was back in Italy admiring the paintings on the walls of the palazzo. And that Vito was by her side.

Her imagination had to be functioning particularly well today, because she could swear she heard his voice behind her.

"I find the still life with fruit paintings particularly compelling, don't you, *cara*?"

Maya didn't dare turn around. Her wishful mind was merely playing tricks on her. She refused to be fooled. No one was behind her. In fact, she was the only person in the hall of this particular gallery.

But the voice somehow continued. "Of course, this one has the added feature of dead birds in the picture. What do you suppose Ruoppolo intended when he included them?"

Maya whirled around so fast her head spun for the briefest second. Then she almost lost her balance completely. For there in front of her, through some miracle, stood Vittorio Rameri. In the flesh. As devilishly handsome as she remembered.

He flashed her a heart-stopping smile.

"Buongiorno, mia vita."

It took several moments before she could get her mouth to work. Her peripheral vision grew dark; the only thing in her focus was the man standing before her. "Vito? Is it really you?"

He spread his arms out, his grin growing wider. "None other."

"But how? What are you doing here?"

"I stopped by the shop first. Talbot's Expert Plumbing. Your uncle told me where I could find you."

Okay. "No, I mean, what are you doing here? In Boston?"

"Ah, see, that question might take a bit of explaining."

"Perhaps you could give me the overall gist."

"Nothing felt right after you left, *cara*. The city I loved suddenly became empty, much smaller all of a sudden once you were gone. Lonelier." He paused to run a finger down her cheek and along her jaw. Her skin warmed wherever he touched it. "Then there was the painting I'd begun of you."

"What about it?"

"I wanted badly to finish work on it, because it reminded me of you. But I couldn't bear to uncover it. Because it reminded me of you."

He stopped speaking and blew out a frustrated breath. "I'm not explaining at all well, am I?"

"No, no. You're doing fine. Don't stop, please."

Vito chuckled then stepped closer to where

she still stood dumbfounded and unable to move so much as a muscle. "I'll do better, *cara*," he said on a soft whisper. "I'll show you."

As he took her in his arms Maya thought for certain none of this could be real. That she was, indeed, going mad. But then Vito took her lips with his and she couldn't think at all.

When they finally parted, Vito drew her even tighter against him, nuzzling his chin against her hair. Then spoke softly on a whisper in her ear in Italian. Maya didn't need a translator to understand his words.

"Ti amo." I love you.

EPILOGUE

"I DON'T KNOW about this, Vito. Last time I attempted getting into one of these things it didn't go so well." Although she *had* ended up meeting Vito as a result.

Still, Maya wasn't so sure a gondola ride was the best way to celebrate the one-year anniversary of the day they'd first met. Vito was trying to be romantic, but all she could focus on was making sure not to reenact the scene where she'd fallen into the water.

"The difference this time is that I'm by your side, *cara*. I won't let you fall."

That wasn't the only difference. "Also, I'm quite sober this time around," she reminded him with a laugh.

Vito hopped into the boat first then helpfully lifted her in. "See? That went pretty smoothly."

"Thank goodness."

She sat next to Vito on the padded seat and

let him pull her into his arms. Slowly, the gondolier began navigating them through the Venice canals.

"Why was it so important that we do this today, anyhow?" Maya asked, though now that the initial boarding was over, she found herself thoroughly enjoying the outing. The splendor of Venetian architecture still took her breath away.

"You need to get used to gondola rides if you're going to be living in Venice part-time."

"I suppose that's fair. After all, you've had to get used to Boston rush-hour traffic."

"Hardly the same."

Maya nestled closer against his length as they approached the waters by St. Mark's and the palazzo. The setting sun had turned the sky above to a striking shade of gold. Moments later, they were heading under the Bridge of Sighs.

"Do you remember the legend I told you about this bridge all those months ago?" Vito asked her.

"I do, as a matter of fact. The legend says that a couple on a gondola as it sails under the Bridge of Sighs will share eternal happiness if they happen to share a kiss just as the bells of St. Mark's Cathedral are ringing."

"Very romantic, *sì*?"

"Yes, it is," Maya agreed. "I also remember discussing that it was statistically almost impossible. Too many random variables."

Vito sighed. "I suppose you're right." He sounded so disappointed that Maya couldn't restrain her laughter. "That doesn't mean we shouldn't try, however," she suggested, not that she needed an excuse to kiss this man.

"Of course, we should. Also, we can create our own little legendary story."

Maya turned in his arms to look at Vito's expression. His mischievous smile and the teasing in his voice told her he was definitely up to something.

"What did you have in mind?"

To her delighted surprise, Vito reached into his pocket and pulled out a small velvet box. Maya's breath left her lungs as he flipped it open to reveal a sparkling square-cut diamond set in a band of pink gold.

"Oh, Vito. It's beautiful."

"Amore mio," he began, "would you do me the honor of becoming my wife?"

She felt the sting of happy tears in her eyes as he slipped the ring on her finger then turned her hand and kissed her palm affectionately.

"Yes! I'd be honored to marry you," Maya managed to blurt out through all the emotion pounding through her heart. Their gondolier turned to give them a whistled cheer.

Vito lifted her chin and brought her face close to his. His lips settled over her own for a long lingering kiss, one that made her blood burn through her veins. Just as she heard the bells of St. Mark's Cathedral ringing through the air.

* * * * *

Welcome to the Destination Brides quartet!

Summer Escape with the Tycoon
by Donna Alward
Swept Away by the Venetian Millionaire
by Nina Singh

*And look out for the next book
Coming soon!*

*And if you enjoyed this story,
check out these other great reads
from Nina Singh*

Captivated by the Millionaire
Christmas with Her Secret Prince
Tempted by Her Island Millionaire

All available now!